THREADS OF A HIGHLAND HEART

WHAT REALLY HAPPENS AFTER 'HAPPILY
EVER AFTER'?

CLAIRE GILLIES

First Paperback Print Edition: 2023 in United Kingdom

Published by Green Isle Publishing

www.clairegillies.com

Paperback ISBN: 978-1-7392452-3-8

Ebook ISBN: 978-1-7392452-4-5

To the Moon

Art thou pale for weariness
Of climbing heaven and gazing on the earth,
Wandering companionless
Among the stars that have a different birth,
And ever changing, like a joyless eye
That finds no object worth its constancy?

-Percy Bysshe Shelley

1

———

Lori pushed away the nervous anticipation that fluttered in her tummy and stepped off the train onto the platform. She wondered if she'd made the right decision?

Should she go back? Hop on the train and head east - return to the exotic countries she'd been enjoying until she felt the pull of home and the guilt of being away from her responsibilities. Living like a nomad with no routines or obligations was thrilling, but no one could live like that forever. It was time to face real life. Back to reality...whatever that meant.

"Are you ok?" Callum tucked a stray hair behind her ear, bringing her focus back to the cold grey day in the Scottish Highlands. The train station was small, its white walls stained a yellow tinge from years of rain. An old man on the other side of the tracks smoked a pipe, wearing a tweed jacket and cap. He saluted them just as a gust of icy wind ran through the station, making Lori squeak. She had her trusty zippy fleece on, which she'd lived in for the last few months, but it was no match for the Scottish weather. The freezing cold got into every nook and cranny; she wasn't sure if she could endure the ten-minute walk home without turning into a block of ice.

Callum didn't wait for her answer, but took her hand in his, leading her into what resembled a blizzard. Lori strode onwards, but her hesitation remained. Back to reality now.

They walked down the open road until they reached a side road which led down into the village. Arlochy, Lori's home, greeted them. Everything in its place just like the day Lori left. Immediately she thought about her mother and father, as she often did when Arlochy was concerned, but she mostly thought of Gran.

After her gran's sudden stroke the previous year, Lori had stayed in Arlochy, leaving her comfortable life in New York. She'd taken the plunge, hoping her move had been the right decision. Her plan had been crystal clear: she would open her own fashion shop and look after Gran. It had taken some convincing – Gran being the independent woman she was and not relying on others for most of her life, Lori had to coax her to accept the idea. An idea that had worked out, to Lori's relief. The pair soon developed a new relationship, much like content housemates rather than testy family members.

Before her travels, Lori had painstakingly organised her two sisters' schedules to keep her gran up to date with doctor's appointments and such. She had left the responsibility to her sisters, another reason it was time to come home to help.

They marched with determination into Arlochy village. The street was hushed, still in the state of slumber it held on to during the winter months. Soon, it would transform when the warmer weather melted the ice, bringing the first wave of tourists. A couple of shops remain open, the grocers and the post office. A necessity for the locals, and for some, the only chance they get to meet for a chat.

The dark swelling sea on the other side of the street captured Lori's attention. A wave crashed over the wooden pier, drenching it in foaming white water. The same spot she and her sisters would leap off on summer nights, shrieking with each jump.

"Plenty of time for all that, darling. Come on, it's freezing!" Callum tugged Lori's hand, leading her onwards for the last few paces until they reached Gran's familiar letterbox. They steered down the lane towards the misshapen house.

"Oh my Lolo!" Gran was the first to come out to greet the new arrivals, her eyes bright but pink with emotion. "I was just coming to pick you up from the station! You walked in this?" She dipped her head and looked up at the flurry. She enveloped Lori in a hug and sniffed back the tears.

"Don't start crying, Gran, or you'll set me off too!"

Gran gripped Lori's hand tightly, taking in her granddaughter's appearance. Gran's white hair rested just above her shoulders in a neat cut; her face, smooth and youthful, from years of healthy eating, and Lori noted, upon reflection, from much rest. Purple spectacles perched on her nose, matching her lavender cropped trousers and blush-pink waterfall cardigan.

Callum kissed Gran on the cheek and hugged her gently. "Don't worry about it, Mary, the train was early. We've hiked in far more extreme conditions than this!" He beamed at her as she patted his cheek with affection.

"Oh, I must hear everything!" Gran enthused. An avid explorer herself, she had travelled the world over, collecting trinkets and adorning her house with her findings.

"Where are your walking sticks, Gran?" Lori gasped, her

tone serious. "We talked about this. You're supposed to use them all the time!"

"Oh hush, child!" Gran waved her hand, while Callum awkwardly collected the bags and went into the house. "You jump to such negative thinking sometimes! I actually came out to surprise you. I don't need the walking sticks... Well, not as much as I did before. I only need them for longer strolls. But around the house I'm fine and dandy!"

Lori eyed her gran with suspicion. "Has the physio confirmed this?"

"Of course! What do you take me for? You think I would just stop using the sticks intentionally?"

Lori considered the question thoughtfully. "Yes, Gran. That's exactly what you would do!"

"Oh wheesht! You can ask the nurse. She'll tell you I'm getting much better." She nodded and put her arm around Lori's shoulder, slowly leading her up the steps and changing the subject with ease. "But first, my dear, we need to get you showered. There's a pungent fragrance emanating from you we shouldn't encourage any longer!"

Bracken, the old collie, had presented himself to Callum, and lay sprawled on the floor in a blissful state. To Lori's annoyance, he ignored her calls; his sole focus on keeping Callum's attention fully on his soft tummy fur. The kitchen was welcomingly cosy as always with jumbles of colourful memorabilia from Gran's travels, along with delicious smells of baking and coffee. Lori opened her backpack on the counter and unwrapped a turquoise plate with intricate black and yellow patterns, relieved to find it still in one piece. She bought it in Sri Lanka, directly from a backstreet potter on her morning rambles. It reminded her of Gran, and she watched the potter mould more clay into vases, with his daughter by his side painting them in fine detail.

The colours complemented the kitchen almost exactly, adding to Gran's style as if it had always been there. Gran carefully placed the large dish high in a glass cupboard door, exhibiting it for all to see, then popped tea bags into her trusty blue spotted teapot. She poured steaming cups of spiced chai tea and Lori smiled, her heart giving an involuntary pang. She was home.

Tammy burst through the door holding two heavily laden plastic bags, and a baby fastened to her chest. She shook the hailstones from her damp hair and set down the bags at the entrance. "What does a girl need to do to get a bit of help round here?" She said breezily and patted the bundle gently.

Callum marched down the hallway and promptly took her bags. "Where's Alan?" He asked, closing the door behind her, the afternoon light already fading to an unhappy gloominess.

"On the boat, of course!" She shook her head. "Well now, won't you give your sister-in-law a kiss?" She winked playfully and patted the baby's bum. "And finally meet your nephew."

Callum diligently obeyed, and Lori ran down the hallway. "Tammy! Oh, and wee Rory!" She wrapped her arms around her sister, laughing as Rory sneezed between them. Tammy expertly unravelled the continuous cloth from around her until Rory's light fuzzy head appeared, with the faint hint of warm red tones the Robertson family were known for. He looked around the room bleary-eyed, eager to get back to his safe haven. Lori lovingly cradled him in her arms, allowing her younger sister to sit down.

"I can't believe you were carrying all those bags, Tam, and him!" Lori nodded to little Rory, who gave her a penetrating look, which if truth be told, made her a little uneasy.

Tam shook her head and arched her back. "It's good for me, it's my exercise."

"You should take it easy, though. I hope those heavy bags aren't on our account?" Lori's attention quickly went back to her nephew as he sighed. "Tam, he is just so beautiful. He's got our hair, that's for sure. Maybe Alan's nose?"

Tammy screwed her own nose. "You haven't seen his enormous feet, those he certainly takes from Alan. I reckon he'll be a big lad." She nodded proudly.

"He's already a big lad!" Callum flexed his fingers for his turn to hold the baby, and with ease gently swayed him in his arms. Rory stared at his new opponent, and Lori smiled as the two boys intently watched one another. Feeling her sister's watchful gaze on her, Tammy gave her a knowing wink that spoke volumes.

"Tam, it's not like you have dainty feet either," Lori scoffed, ignoring any assumptions her sister may have.

"Hey!" Tammy punched her big sister's shoulder with a strength Lori hadn't expected.

"I can see I might need to up my game in the whole exercise department if I'm not wanting to be bullied by my younger sis!"

"Ha! Me bully you? Chance would be a fine thing!" Tammy shooed them away and unpacked vegetables, while Gran uncharacteristically went to bed until dinner was ready.

Callum played with Rory, supporting the little boy's chubby arms and bobbing him gently on his knee. Lori quietly endured a wide range of emotions watching the man she loved holding a baby for the first time. They'd been together less than a year, but their connection ran deep. After being high school sweethearts many years prior, she was in some ways still getting to know him as the man he had become. It hadn't crossed her mind to wonder if Callum even liked babies! He had been attentive to Lori's nieces, Maggie and Anne. But they were independent, mischievous pre-tween girls. Not babies. Lori watched Callum's expression, his face radiating a peaceful joy, which after months of travelling together, she hadn't witnessed.

"How is Gran?" Lori asked in hushed tones.

Tammy held a large sharp knife and carved a butternut squash. Lori noticed her sister's eye dart from Gran's room, to Rory, then back to Lori, all in a split second, no doubt her multitasking skills would have graduated a notch since becoming a mum. Tammy clicked on the oven and drizzled oil over the chopped squash. She pulled out a pot from the bottom cupboard, filled it with water, and cast Lori a glance, processing her question. She lit the gas cooker and prepared pasta.

"She said the nurse cleared her."

Tammy blinked at Lori and chopped onions. "No, she's not 'cleared', but the nurse said she's getting better. She's been amazing with Rory. I've been able to crash here since Alan's been away..." She stopped short, a strange look in her eyes. "I really think she's on the mend, no doubt about it."

"And you don't think she's taking on too much?"

"No, at least I don't think so... I try to do as much as I can, cook, clean when Rory is sleeping, and..." Her tone suddenly hurt, she turned away to put the lid on the pot of hot water.

"I don't mean that, Tammy, you are doing loads! You have got Rory and I'm so sorry I wasn't here for the start of things."

Tammy shrugged, her hand gripping the knife.

"But I'm here now," Lori gave an encouraging smile, "and I will take over anything that needs doing. Honestly,

Tam, you've done so much. I can take Gran to appointments and cook and clean. Anything else I can do, just let me know."

Tammy nodded. Her eyes drifted over to Callum. "You might have enough work to do soon enough. Looks like someone might be broody," she whispered next to Lori's ear as Callum pointed out the yellow daffodils sprouting in the garden to Rory.

"No, don't be silly. He's more brooding than broody." Lori chuckled at her poor joke and swiped a piece of crusty bread from the chopping board.

Tammy raised her eyebrows. "I know that look. That's the look of heartache and longing all wrapped into one. Trust me, that man wants children."

Lori immediately put down the crust, her stomach lurching. She froze by the kitchen counter, a tightness rising in her throat. Not as intense as her old panic attacks used to be, but still an unpleasant sensation.

Tammy watched Lori carefully. "You have spoken about these things, right? I mean, you're not getting any younger. If you want to have kids, you'll need to plan."

"It's fine, Tammy, we're good. There's nothing to worry about," Lori said quickly, eager to change the subject.

Callum lifted Rory high in the air to the sound of aeroplane noises and Tammy pressed her lips together, suppressing a chuckle. "OK, OK, I'm just saying, your twenties are for having the career, the one-night stands, the fun. Your thirties are for having kids."

Lori sighed heavily, suddenly depressed beyond belief. "And your forties?"

"Um... I'm not sure, ask me when I'm forty!" Tammy said breezily and stirred the pasta, oblivious to her sister's newfound dilemma.

2

Lori's nieces, Maggie and Anne, ran through the front door, wrapping their arms around their beloved aunt. She beamed at them, her heart swelling. She had come so close to leaving them behind for her life in New York. Having been a constant presence in their lives before embarking on her travels with Callum, she already yearned to spend more time with them.

"I drew you a picture." Maggie produced a brightly coloured sketch with smiling faces and obscure objects. "There's the rainbow, there's Daddy on his boat, there's you on the beach with me building sandcastles, and Mum and Karen are swimming in the sea with big blobby jellyfish everywhere!" Maggie said animatedly. She handed her art over proudly to her aunt, who admired it and secured it on the fridge.

"Where am I?" Anne, the older sibling, nudged Maggie.

Maggie screwed up her nose and, with a critical eye over her work, shrugged. "You're swimming in the sea too... you're just diving underneath somewhere," she said matter-of-factly, her attention quickly grabbed by Bracken. The lazy dog sat between the girls, waiting for his petting ritual to begin.

"You look great, Lo." Jean opened her arms to hug her sister. Her partner Karen, hovering behind, held onto a bottle of wine and a three-tiered cake.

"Thanks, sis. Oh, you baked, Karen, you really shouldn't have!" Lori's appetite returned upon seeing a thick iced chocolate cake with cream oozing at the sides.

"Well, it's a special celebration, isn't it? Plus, it gives me something else to do other than study the whole time!" Karen placed the treats on the counter. Since Karen and Callum's business, Adventurous Tours, ended by mutual agreement, Karen had returned to school.

Callum appeared on the scene bobbing Rory up and down in his arms, and for a moment, all chatter ceased. Lori knew Jean's eyes were on her, trying her best to contain herself. Lori had a good mind to make a joke about their reactions, by poking fun at them all. What was wrong with them? Couldn't a man hold a baby without all the women of the house losing their minds?

Before Lori could say anything, Tammy announced dinner was ready. With much fuss and commotion, the family seated themselves around the dining table.

Tammy placed garlic bread, roast vegetables, pasta, and an enormous pot of rich bolognese sauce on the table. "Right, every woman for herself." She smiled, shaking her head. "Sorry, Callum, what I mean is, everyone dig in!"

Gran stood up slowly, while everyone was helping themselves. "Now you know I'm not one for speeches..."

Lori coughed, trying not to laugh. Gran often started a speech this way. For someone who "wasn't one for speeches," she sure liked to make them. Her gran raised an eyebrow, silencing her granddaughter immediately.

Gran tapped her glass to command more attention over the drone of her great-granddaughters fighting over the garlic bread. Jean whipped the item causing such chaos between Maggie and Anne and put it on her own plate. Gran clasped her hands, patiently waiting for the little ones to finish squabbling. Once the room fell silent, she beamed at her family before her.

"It's so wonderful to have you all here again. Sadly Alan is working, but, Tam, we're all here to help. Rory, what a strong wee lad. He's an angel come into our lives."

"He's as good as gold." Tammy admired her bundle of joy who snoozed on a day cot in the corner.

"And of course, Lori and Callum," Gran nodded. "We're all delighted that you're both finally home. I can now ease off on the prayers and sprinkling holy water on your photo in the lounge." She gestured to the framed picture she had taken of Lori and Callum before their travels. In the photo, they clung to each other by the garden shed, their forced smiles revealing Gran's lack of photography skills.

Jean scoffed, and Lori casually nudged her in the ribs. Their gran may have traveled the world, but she was a serious worrier and would resort to over-the-top measures, like holy water. Lori was certain that Father Angus would be relieved to know they were finally home. She had no doubt that her Gran hassled the poor priest daily, demanding his prayers on their behalf.

Gran raised her eyebrow in Jean's direction, not paying too much attention. "Anyway, we missed you and can't wait to hear your special news."

Unsure of Gran's remark, Lori exchanged a glance with Callum, whose blank expression met hers.

"I meant to say your travelling news, your adventures! We want to hear that news," Gran corrected herself quickly.

"You know I was in Hong Kong once too. I'd never walked so much in my life!" She chuckled to herself. "Anyway, I digress. I dare say you'll both be onto the next adventure soon... Whatever that might be." She gave a knowing nod to Callum and raised her glass. "To the returned travellers, may you know in your heart that no matter where you go, this is always home."

"Hear! hear!" Jean agreed with vigour and split the last piece of garlic bread, giving it back to both her daughters.

"Auntie Lori?" Anne gripped a knife and fork tightly, her elbows on the table. "Auntie Karen says you saw huge whales in the ocean?" Anne asked quietly, her eyes keen. Lori's older niece was more studious than Maggie, who had an energy that never disappeared.

"We did. We saw one of the rarest whales out there, the blue whale!"

Anne's face lit up. "They are big, like as big as..." She considered for a moment.

"Three school buses, all lined up one after the other!" Callum chimed in. "Pretty big, eh?"

Anne smiled, her face full of wonder. "Wow!"

"The biggest animal in the entire world!" Lori playfully nudged her niece on the shoulder. "When you're older, maybe you'll see one too!"

"When I'm older, I'm going to travel the universe!" Maggie exclaimed, raising her hands in the air, capturing the room's attention, diverting it from her sister.

Anne nodded. "I'm going to be an explorer too, maybe a writer, a teacher like Mummy and a—"

"Well, I'm going to be a teacher like Mummy too," Maggie interrupted, then briefly considered the statement and added, "also a policewoman, a pop star and a fairy!"

Everyone at the table roared with laughter, and Maggie

piped up even louder, "and a lighthouse keeper and a fisherman!"

"Well, that's sweet, darlings, that you want to be a teacher like me, as long as you are sensible headed and you follow your heart... you can do anything in this life." She exchanged a loving look with Karen next to her and Karen placed her hand gently over Jean's. The gesture was more than the family had witnessed before, and Lori looked away, unsure if she was trespassing in an intimate moment.

Lori lay wide awake in bed, the house's stillness shattered by sporadic bursts of crying from Rory in Tammy's temporary room. Each sharp cry made Lori wince, yet the ensuing silence suggested that Tammy was attentively caring for him throughout the night.

The thought of having someone so dependent on her weighed on Lori's mind. While she recognised the beauty of such a bond, she also acknowledged its demanding nature. The idea of enduring the little sleep Tammy was currently experiencing seemed unimaginable to Lori. Her freedom was precious, especially after her decision to leave New York for Arlochy. She was at a stage in her life where she didn't want to be overworked and overstressed. The years of panic attacks had plagued her because she couldn't say no. Now that she had reclaimed her freedom, she was determined not to part with it so soon.

Restlessly, Lori shifted in bed and kicked her leg out from under the covers. Callum, still drowsy, draped an arm over her and snuggled into the back of her neck.

"Everything OK?" he murmured in her ear.

"Everything's fine. Go back to sleep. I'm going to get a

glass of water." Lori turned to kiss him gently on the lips before slipping out from the warmth of his body. She watched him fall instantly back to sleep, and her heart jolted just thinking of how close they had been to losing each other. Just as she had almost left her nieces forever, she had almost left him too – a decision she knew she would have regretted for the rest of her life. But she had come to her senses. She chose Callum, and he was her world. With the best man she ever knew at her side, she felt capable of anything.

Lori wandered out to the kitchen and rummaged in the fridge for something, but she didn't know what. She padded barefoot across the dimly lit kitchen and past Bracken, who lay in his bed by the glass sliding door, keeping a lazy eye on her. She petted him briefly and ventured out onto the veranda overlooking the garden. The full moon illuminated the sky, flooding the landscape with bright light. Lori heard another faint whimper from Rory inside, along with the gentle rustle of trees. The wind blew through her, refreshing her body and bringing her senses alive. She needed to be somewhere, do something with her energy. But where could she go? The sensible voice inside her suggested returning to her warm bed; morning was approaching, and a new day with its accompanying distractions lay ahead. But something nagged within her. She gritted her teeth against the cool wind and looked up at the moon. It was smiling down at her. As she had always known it to do; a joyful face carved out in the glowing light. Even as a little girl, he remained there. Her friend in the dark, guiding her home safely. *The man on the moon.* It followed her, casting its watchful gaze and offering a knowing grin, as if in possession of her secrets, silently accompanying her on her journey.

But tonight she didn't feel reassured. She could feel

something else: smugness. An almost challenging smile. Provoking her.

"What?" She asked him defiantly. But, of course, he made no reply. How could he? He was the moon, after all. What had she expected? That he would beam her up and they'd have a chat?

Lori regarded the faint shadows on his milky surface. "Well, I'll show you, Mr Moon," she whispered.

She wasted no time, giving Bracken a final pat before quietly snatching a spare coat by the front door and slipping on her wellies. Her feet guided her toward the pier, taking charge before her mind could fully process the unfolding events. The moon cast its illuminating glow, enhancing the entire village. Ahead, Lori's gaze fell upon the shuttered bookshop, its shelves lined with ageing novels, a playful cat darting across the street, and the familiar sight of the red fishing boat anchored off the coast. Lori's skin tingled in the chilly breeze as a surge of excitement ran through her. She reached the pier edge and glanced around to be sure no accidental onlookers were there. She was alone. Free. She removed her coat, shivering in her thin t-shirt and knickers, and braced herself for what lay ahead. And just like she did as a girl, a quick intake of breath and, without further thought, she plunged headlong into the bitterly cold water. A yelp escaped her at the shock of what felt like a thousand knives. She surfaced, pushing back her heavy hair, her legs kicking, keeping her afloat. Adrenaline hit her, and the immediate agony of the cold subsided, leaving a stinging sensation. A deliciousness enveloped her as she glided through the calm dark water. She watched the moon high above, the Milky Way trailing across the skyline and at that moment a clarity came over her. Lori basked in the beauty surrounding her. Where she had been in life led her here. Back home.

She made a deal with the sea. Wherever life took her, this was who she was, her roots were here.

The moon's hue captured her attention once more. His smirk now relaxed, but still watching her intently. She then made a deal with the man on the moon. Whatever challenges he threw at her, she wouldn't give in so easily.

3

A few miles west from Arlochy stood the ferry town of Morvaig, a hub of activity in the summer months, but as it was only spring, the tourists were low in numbers. Lori strolled through its small streets, taking in the charming seaside shops and the town's renowned fish and chip cafes. She couldn't help her excitement bubbling inside her as her little shop came into view. The boutique stood out with its freshly painted white wall and nautical blue window and front door, neatly nestled between the other shop fronts. Lori felt a wave of pride. *This is my boutique.* She admired the window display. Warm light highlighted well-dressed mannequins with sprigs of white and pink blossom branches positioned around the edges. Everything looked fresh; spring was here. One mannequin lounged on a wooden chair, wearing a loose kimono Lori had made from grey wool with an appliqué of birds and ivy in bright colours. The other reached up to a branch in a high-waisted tartan mini skirt along with a cream polo neck. Lori would not have positioned them in such a way, or mixed such different styles, but it screamed a certain chic and cultured aesthetic that looked inviting.

Lori opened the door slowly, savouring the moment, the bell tickling above.

"It is a good fit. I'm telling you, Diane, you wear this to the Hunters' tea party and you will be the belle of the ball. Or should I say the belle of the buffet!" Rhona clasped her hands together, admiring her customer, who twisted and turned in a cream velvet coat. It fastened at the waist and tapered out in a full skirt, skimming just under her knees. Rhona glanced at Lori briefly with a coy wink, but quickly brought her attention back to the customer.

Diane looked at her reflection, moving this way and that, her expression uncertain. "I like it, but I'm not so sure. Maybe the yellow one was better? Although..."

"Of course, the daffodil yellow is stunning. Really brings out your eyes. But this one does wonders for your skin. You are positively glowing, Diane." Rhona tapped her finger gently on her chin, studying the garment before her.

"Thank you." Diane nodded graciously, accepting the compliment. "I was in Barbados last month."

"Barbados, I should be so lucky!" Rhona cried. "If only! Crystal-clear water and shimmering sunshine. Yes, please!"

Diane nodded in agreement, her focus still on her reflection.

"Well, perhaps you have another occasion you could wear the yellow? If only I could have your social life, Diane, I'd have this coat in every colour – that's the beauty of it, you see – it's classic, sophisticated. Would you like me to pack them both for you?" Rhona flicked her wrist and smoothed her hand over the back seam of the cream coat, watching Diane with admiration in the mirror. "One thing is for certain, you'll be wearing a truly unique item, Diane."

Rhona skirted around the counter, pulling out a gold ribbon and other gift-wrapping materials.

"Oh, what the heck!" Fumbling in her handbag, Diane pulled out a credit card. "That husband of mine is always on business trips, living the life of Riley, so I should be able to treat myself from time to time!" She chuckled, patting her expensive ash blonde bob-cut.

Rhona artfully folded the garments in tissue paper before tying a large satin bow on top. With a last flourish, she handed Diane a black bag, exposing the embossed gold letters on its side: "Couturier by the Pier", Lori's fashion label. A brand only recently created, which sent tingles down her spine witnessing it as a bystander.

To Lori's relief, Rhona had agreed to mind the shop for two days a week while she was travelling. Otherwise, her new business would have been closed for the winter months. Lori knew that at such an early stage it was crucial to raise brand awareness and was keen for any able body to help her. Little did she realise Rhona wasn't just able, she was the perfect person; her skills in sales alone were apparent, for little stock remained on the shelves.

"Well well, the wanderer returns!" Rhona pulled Lori in for a hug when the door tinkled on Diane's departure.

"Rhona, you're amazing. I can't believe you just sold two of my most expensive coats to one woman!" Lori had made only a small selection of one-off coats and cringed at how much she needed to charge for them. She lacked the gumption to sell them, preferring to hide behind her sewing machine if any customers showed interest.

"Oh, those babies sell themselves! The work you put into them, Diane got a good deal!" Rhona flicked her short dark hair back playfully.

"Still, you are a dark horse. I never knew you were a first-class saleswoman." Lori admitted with a bemused smile. She had secretly monitored Rhona's social media posts for *Couturier by the Pier* on the rare occasions she had Wi-Fi, if she wasn't in a jungle or a remote island. But the boutique suited Rhona in a way Lori didn't expect; she was a natural.

"I quite enjoy it, actually. It beats doing housework and nagging the kids to clean up after themselves! My mum is on babysitting duty!" She nodded with a grin, resting her hand on the counter. "Honestly, it's been lovely just getting on that ferry, having a cup of coffee and knowing I've got a few hours to meself. Oh, and of course catching up on all the latest gossip!" She gasped, her eyes suddenly wide. "Oh, and I hope you don't mind, I made a few changes around here?" She bit her lip and scrunched her nose.

"Well, if it's anything like the window display, you've done a great job." Lori beamed.

"Good holiday?" Rhona winked. Changing the subject at rapid speed was a particular trait of hers. She often complained there were never enough hours in the day to talk, or in this case, tap her friend for information.

"It was travelling, so you know, hiking, roughing it, that kind of thing. So not really a holiday."

"Sounds wonderful," Rhona said flatly.

"It was." Lori breathed. She had spent the better part of the trip at Callum's side. They had been inseparable. Rekindling their love in unusual surroundings; nights together listening to the waves in Con Dao, mornings buzzing through busy streets on a motorbike in Colombo. It had been carefree, a little too carefree at times – she would not be disclosing too much information to Gran. They both revisited their younger selves, kayaking by day and making love throughout the night. Lori had never felt so connected to anything in her whole life, until Callum came back to her.

"And Callum?" Rhona interrupted Lori's thoughts. "They say 'a couple who travel together, stay together.'" Rhona folded the remaining tissue paper and stashed it back under the counter before her eagle eye was back on Lori again.

"Everyone is eager to know if we argued much or split up multiple times!" She shook her head. "Truth is, we had the best time. I'm sorry to disappoint you all." She raised her chin, laughing at Rhona's outrage.

"Well well, we all want the best for you both. I just know that if I went on a holiday to Corfu with hubby and the family, I'd be more stressed than relaxed! No thanks!"

"That's because you have kids in the mix, Rhona. If it was just you and Malcolm, you wouldn't want to leave the hotel so easily. Next time, get your mum to look after the wee scamps!"

"Our dirty weekends are long gone, Lo. If I presented the idea to Malcolm, he would give me a list of reasons why not to. The first five hundred of them being the farm!" Rhona had married her long-term boyfriend Malcolm when Lori was a junior secretary in Australia. She'd been the first of her peers to get married, which Lori, being an early twenty-something, would have avoided like the plague.

"Oh, I'm sure he'd be dead keen to whisk you away. Just elaborate that it's the big 'DW' and I'm sure he'd take over the preparations!" A cackle escaped Lori, and she covered her mouth in shock.

"DW?" Rhona frowned.

"Dirty Weekend!"

Rhona raised her eyebrows, her expression less than playful. "After having kids – there's a lot you don't know – let's just say the mood isn't so sexy. For him and me! You'll know once you have some."

Lori felt immediately on the spot and shook off the icy shiver that trailed up her spine.

Rhona folded her arms, and a frown line appeared on her forehead that Lori hadn't seen before. "I'm sure things will sort themselves out."

Before Lori could ask her friend to elaborate, the subject was changed in classic Rhona style.

"Lori darling, your hair. Did you get dreadlocks or something?" She tapped the side of her mouth and shook her head disapprovingly. "You look like someone pulled you through a bush. I *knew* Callum was a mad thing in the sack!" A slow smile spread over her face. "I can't believe your gran let you in the house like that. Go see Katie down the road." She shooed Lori away. "No one's going to take you seriously as a fashionista looking like you just stepped off Pirates of the Caribbean! Go this instant!"

Lori self-consciously walked to the hairdressers, her coat wrapped around her ears shielding her from the wind, and any disapproving eyes. Since being told by not one but two people of her shabby appearance, she wondered just how bad she looked. Messy chic could be a thing. She could make it a thing.

But rather than encourage that idea, she dashed into the hairdressers.

Two cups of tea and all the celebrity gossip she could read later, Lori emerged from Katie's, her hair detangled and a little shorter than before. No one could accuse her of being dragged through a bush again!

Rhona had waved her farewells to catch the ferry home, and Lori took the time to become reacquainted with the shop. She breathed in the comforting smell of wool fabrics and the remains of Rhona's citrus perfume. She felt dizzy with enthusiasm... or perhaps it was the effects of the perfume! Lori hummed to herself, adjusting the music on the sound system to an upbeat folk tune and cast her eyes around the shop, looking for inspiration. She was low on capes, dress coats, skirts, and waistcoats, which she jotted down on her to-do list and continued to rifle through the rails. One thing was for sure, Lori needed to produce stock immediately! From underneath her large cutting table she pulled out a roll of dark navy wool and unravelled it, smoothing it with her hand for any kinks or creases. Then, with determination, she selected a few cardboard patterns from her collection in the back cupboard. All of which were beautifully organised by size and style, secured on hooks and waiting for her attention. She placed pattern cut-outs on fabric, traced around them in bright pink chalk, and with huge tailor's shears, cut into the thick wool with a satisfying crunch. Lori found this part of the process the most fulfilling; seeing the flat piece of cloth beginning to take shape, like she was coaxing it into being. Someone would wear whatever these would soon become, perhaps for a special occasion, and hopefully love them as a keepsake. She was creating, giving a lease on life that wasn't there before. In a strange way, they felt like her babies, her creations, her love.

Lost in a trance, Lori remained oblivious to the tinkle of the doorbell and the giggles of the surrounding audience, a group of teenage girls in school uniforms.

"Come in, girls. Please look around. Don't mind me, I get a little distracted." Lori waved at them but remained focused cutting more fabric.

One girl, with thick luscious blonde locks, rocked back on her heels, glancing at the few items on display. "You don't have much," she remarked, chewing gum. Lori caught her making a face at her friend, who sniggered under her breath.

"No," Lori said breezily, not succumbing to the teenager's smugness. "But that's why I'm making more." She threw another piece of chopped fabric onto a pile, scissors still in her hand. "You go to Morvaig high school, then?"

The sniggering friend continued, apparently the only contribution she could make. The girl with the gum squinted at Lori's table full of fabric. "You make the clothes?"

"I sure do!" Lori placed the used cardboard patterns back onto hangers and stretched to hang them in the back cupboard.

"It's like for older women?... maybe older than my mum," the blonde teen mused, flashing her friends an expression Lori couldn't make out.

"Well, I wouldn't say that—"

"We must get back to school, right?" The blonde leader of the pack flicked her hair, and the gang shuffled out the door after her.

"Rude little..." Lori crossed her arms, watching the door slam behind them, stunned at how brazen teenagers were these days. She raised her eyebrows and exhaled. Her gran would have zapped any unruly behaviour before it developed. Mary Robertson may be the gentlest of souls, but she had a grit within her no one dared challenge.

Lori turned back to the mounds of neatly cut fabric and stacked them beside her large sewing machine at the far end of the shop. When she started her business, Lori initially utilised her mother's antique Singer sewing machine to create most of the items. However, as her shop expanded, she purchased her very own heavy-duty sewing machine and retired her mother's. The retired machine now served as a decorative element, displayed on the wall amidst shelves of neatly folded tweed fabrics arranged in a gradient of colours resembling a rainbow. Above, framed photographs of her mother and grandmother proudly adorned the wall, serving as her daily inspiration and silent motivators.

As the door tinkled once again, a different schoolgirl appeared in the doorway, setting her apart from the others. With an upright posture and a high up-do of raven black hair, she exuded a distinctive presence. Unlike her predecessors, she donned black trousers, a black waistcoat, and a matching black jacket. The weight of her heavy bag was the only indication that she was, indeed, a school student. She cleared her throat. "Can I look around?"

"Of course, please," Lori welcomed her in with a wave. "You missed your friends. They left a few minutes ago."

"Oh, they're not my friends." She swallowed, gently touching some scarves by the door, still uncertain to cross the threshold.

Lori watched the girl, her eager eyes taking in the clothing on display, then she gasped. "Is that...it looks like Christian Dior?" She weaved between the railings and cautiously moved around the mannequin tucked in the corner. Her fingers gently caressed a cream silk jacket over a billowing black skirt underneath. Her face flushed, her interest piqued.

"Inspired by Dior, yes." Lori grinned, impressed at the girl's astute fashion knowledge. "You like Dior?"

"Yes, well, he was revolutionary. Before him, designers used very little fabric because of the war. He revived haute couture in Paris!" She looked back at the dress. "This is breathtaking." Her shy countenance disappeared the more she examined the garment.

Lori waved the compliment away, still unsure of her capabilities as a designer. "I just felt inspired. Anyway, it's a bit too dramatic for anyone around here. Can you really see a local wearing this to pop out for a carton of milk?" Lori scoffed. "This is just a statement piece, but my bread and butter is the everyday wear." She swiped a loose hair from a maroon blazer next to her.

"If I could, I would make these..." The teen pointed to the cream silk jacket. "You never know where it might lead you." Her wide eyes adjusted back to Lori's. "I mean, that's what I would do." She shrugged and pursed her lips. "Thanks for letting me look around."

"Anytime!" Lori waved to the young girl who left just as quietly as she came in.

Lori turned back to the work before her and sighed. She popped on the kettle in the back kitchenette, needing her caffeine hit to get her through the graft ahead. As the kettle bubbled, Lori craned her neck back toward the elaborate style in the corner. Mug in hand, she scrutinised the outfit from a distance. She'd embroidered a delicate black rose design on each button. The process had taken her several nights, but the result was effective. But to what end? It was a pretty piece that would likely remain in the same spot for another year before going into storage. She needed to be realistic. She lived in a rural town, not a trendy part of London. No one would pay for anything like this. While it certainly caught attention, customers would simply take a brief look at the price tag before promptly distancing themselves from it.

Lori couldn't blame them. It was how things were here.

She stirred her coffee and took a sip. The strong flavour

spurred her onwards, and she wasted no time in stitching fabric. The machine buzzed loudly, tapping in time to the fast music playing overhead. Lori welcomed the trance-like state and stitched wools together; royal blue wool and grey herringbone zipped through, passing under the needle at rapid speed. She let her mind wander as her hands and feet continued. But soon without thinking, her foot gently eased off the treadle, and she glanced back at the Dior style jacket. A futile thought perhaps, but she couldn't help but wonder if could she make something else like it?

4

"Are you pulling another all-nighter?" Callum massaged Lori's shoulders, making her sigh with relief. The harsh light of her sewing machine had made her eyes strain, and she sat back, giving in to Callum's touch.

"I think you need some help, Lori, you can't put in these hours all the time." His cool hand gently touched her temples as he leaned down to kiss her. "And I want to see my woman, our bed is cold without you." He spread his hands back over her shoulders and she sighed again. Lori had worked late in the shop for the last week; her days had been a blur of assisting customers, meaning the only time she could produce any work was after opening hours. The little work she did finish was purchased immediately, a good problem to have, she told herself, but how was she ever going to get enough stock? At this rate, she'd only have the expensive cream jacket and skirt gathering dust in the corner, pressuring every customer who set foot in the shop to buy it!

"I will. It's just difficult to get any helpers," she

murmured as he kissed her neck, then shook herself awake. "And I'm not 'your woman', Callum, you don't own me," she retorted, breaking free from his touch.

"Don't I know that?" A smile spread across his face. "But the bed *is* cold, that much is true."

Lori looked at the many unfinished cups of coffee dotted around, leaving their sticky brown rings on surfaces. She needed a break. She wasn't that twenty-something girl full of boundless energy who could happily work late, party hard, then repeat the process the next day.

Callum was right, of course. There was no point in exhausting herself soon after she returned home. She needed to come up with ideas.

After sitting upright all day, her body drooped in the sewing chair. Callum positioned his arms underneath her, providing support as she rose from her chair. Then, without any warning, he effortlessly lifted her high in the air, as if bench pressing her. The suddenness of the movement startled Lori, causing her to let out a startled shriek. "Put me down! You'll drop me!"

"Well, what would you like, my darling, put down or dropped?" He strained, his face turning a little pink, but continued to hold her.

"Callum, you'll hurt yourself! Please put me down!" Laughter escaped from Lori, unable to contain her amusement. Even if it meant potential harm to himself, Callum's determination to bring a smile to her face had worked. Lori wriggled out of his grip and playfully shoved him. She looked at the mess across the shop floor – fabric cuttings were everywhere, and a pile of half-made skirts lay strewn across the cutting table and thrown across already heavily laden rails. She needed to make some decisions. At this rate, her venture wasn't sustainable, even with her drive and ambition. Lori shut her eyes at the mess. *Let it wait till tomor-row.* She laid her head on Callum's shoulder, his woody scent enticing her. She switched off the light, locked the door, and was led home to the promise of a hot shower and a snuggle in bed with the man she loved.

Rhona showed up the next morning, wearing a black suit jacket, her hair straightened to perfection. She removed her sunglasses and threw her handbag on the cutting table. "Now, what's all this about a business meeting, darling?" She exuded a confidence that left Lori almost tongue-tied.

"Oh, um... well, I thought we might have a chat."

Rhona rolled her eyes and leaned on the workbench. "Here was me thinking something mighty important was going to be discussed here without delay. I am a very important lady with little time for chitchats, you know!"

Lori clasped her hands tightly. Her thoughts immediately drifted to her old boss, Frankie, and the fast-paced office life she endured. Frankie had been her mentor, but whose directness and authority had been both unnerving and admirable.

"Oh gawd! Lori, I'm just messing!" Rhona laughed with her whole body and dabbed her eyes. "You should see your face!"

"Bloody hell, I thought you'd had a brain transplant last night. Or changed personality on the ferry over. You look impressive, though!" Lori relaxed her shoulders. The lasting effect of her demanding and pressured old life still lingered in the back of her mind.

"Yes, I know." Rhona rummaged in her bag for her hand mirror to check her appearance.

Lori moved towards the kitchenette and poured tea into two mugs; one covered in kiwi fruit and one with a pink hen, both pilfered from her gran's collection. She splashed a drop of milk in each and handed one to Rhona, who wiped a fleck of mascara from under her eye.

"Oh, thanks, darling. You seemed so cryptic on the phone, but you said 'business meeting?' So don't let a girl get all dressed up for nothing!" Rhona scoffed.

Lori got straight to the point. "I want to offer you a job. You were amazing while I was away, and I know that was only as a favour, but I would really love to have you with me here at the shop." Lori watched Rhona's expression carefully. She'd known her since high school, but just like her relationship with Callum, she had only recently rekindled their friendship. She hoped her gut was right to bring her friend into business with her.

Rhona nodded slowly, her eyes glistening. "I thought perhaps you were going to ask me to cover the shop again." She placed her mug down, her hand clenched into a fist on her chest. "Really? You want me to work here?"

"Of course I do!" Lori exclaimed. On most days, customers had searched for Rhona, only to be left disappointed when she was nowhere to be found. After witnessing her friend's exceptional talents in sales, Lori would have defended Rhona fiercely against anyone attempting to recruit her. Rhona was a hidden gem, a rare find waiting to be discovered, and she remained blissfully unaware of her own potential. "I know you have the kids, so whatever days... hours you could do, I'll happily work around you. That is..." She paused. "If you want the job?"

Rhona narrowed her eyes and tapped her newly rouged lips with a pensive pause. Then abruptly hooted and hugged her friend. "I would love to work here!" She bounced on the spot. "I can say I work for 'Couturier by the Pier', darling. A high-end fashion brand! It certainly has a nice ring to it!" She squealed. "But I have the kids to think of. Maybe I can get my mum to help, or Malcolm can do something other than the farm..." she mumbled.

"I don't want to stress you, but I really want you to come and be a part of the shop. I'll work around you and I want to pay you, of course." Lori had already devised a plan and worked out the costs of bringing on staff. She confirmed the wage she could pay Rhona.

"At that price, the kids will mind themselves!" Rhona laughed. "I'm joking, of course, but are you sure? Can you afford that?"

Lori's confidence only grew stronger as her friend questioned the salary. It confirmed that Rhona was the perfect accomplice to have in the business, someone who cared about the financial aspects and wasn't afraid to ask the tough questions. Lori pulled out an already chilled bottle of bubbly from the kitchen fridge in anticipation of Rhona's acceptance.

"It's only just past midday!" Rhona laughed and sat at the till, stretching out her legs. "You are a bad influence, Lori Robertson, you always were!"

"Hey, it was you who was the bad influence! I would have been the nicest girl in high school!" She snorted, thinking of the teen girls who came in some days before.

"Nice is boring. We had some fun times though, didn't we?" She caught Lori's eye as she grabbed her glass. "What will we toast to?" She sat up, her glass held high.

"To friendship, taking chances and new beginnings. Here's to a fun summer!"

The two clinked and in a sea of high spirits reminisced their youth and looked to an exciting future that lay ahead.

Lori left Rhona to close up the shop. She had already started making a list of ideas and improvements to the shop front, which Lori welcomed. If she could focus on designing and making the products, Rhona could manage the boutique. It might just work! Lori passed by the other shops en route to her car, saluting fellow business owners on the windy street. She strutted in her own made burnt orange wrap coat, feeling an overwhelming sense of belonging. At the end of the street, a bouquet of bright flowers caught her eye, and on impulse, she gathered the most vibrant bunch for her grandmother.

Finishing work early had made her want to do something else on her way home, so she pulled in at a nearby beach and walked along the shoreline in the biting cold wind. Kicking the sand underneath her boots, she took a deep breath in and gazed out to islands ahead. The beach was empty, other than a mother and toddler near the water's edge. The woman supported the little babe with outstretched arms, encouraging them to walk. A trickle of tide came in and she picked up the child, spinning them around in shrieks of delight. Lori smiled at the pair as she passed, the little one bundled up in a hat and a woolly outfit, who babbled to their mother with conviction. Lori squinted as the sun shimmied its way out from the clouds and pierced the water. The vast beach stretched out, meeting the teal blue sea. She turned back to see the pair retreating to their parked car and felt a tinge of disappointment. She turned her gaze back to the horizon, allowing the wild wind to blow away the jumbled emotions inside her.

5

Tammy reluctantly crawled out of bed, feeling the weight of the late morning. Her mind was already consumed by thoughts of Rory, who lay sleeping beside her. It was nothing short of a miracle considering the night they both had, but she assumed he must be exhausted from all the crying. Tammy carefully crept past him, trying not to disturb his slumber, and almost made it to the bathroom where she yearned for a hot shower, but as if sensing her presence, Rory's head moved from side to side, and soon he let out a familiar cry. With a sigh, Tammy picked him up, determined not to let her mood be dampened today. While she might not manage to have a shower by herself, she was resolute to have one, one way or another.

Today was a special day; she would be seeing Alan. Her heart raced at the thought. It had been over a week since he had been on dry land, and this time she wanted to make an effort.

After attending to Rory's needs and dressing him in a fresh outfit, Tammy secured him in a bouncer chair on the bathroom floor. His eyes widened as the lullaby music played, soothing him. Tammy couldn't help but gaze at him as she lathered herself with hot, soapy water. But how she welcomed the delicious luxury of a shower. The warm water cascaded over her body, and she took special care to shave areas she had neglected for far too long. It had been an eternity since she had truly looked at herself since childbirth.

Rory started to fuss, so she hurriedly washed her hair, and stepped out of the shower, before his crying escalated. Before she could reach for a towel, she caught a glimpse of herself in the mirror. Her heart sank. Her once perky breasts now hung heavy, like oversized sacks grazing the top of her belly. Red angry stretch marks adorned her thighs and stomach, and unfamiliar jiggles teased her every movement. Would she ever get her figure back? Tammy had always prided herself on being busy, always on the go. But after having Rory, everything came to a halt, and some days she didn't even leave the house.

Gran tapped on the door, holding out a cup of tea, and took Rory away so Tammy could get ready. Tammy rummaged through her wardrobe, but she realised she didn't have many options. Eventually, she settled on a pair of loose trousers, a cream blouse, and the same cardigan she had been wearing since Alan's departure.

Alan wouldn't notice.

Tammy spent extra time moisturising her body, hoping that with each rub, her stretch marks would disappear. She pulled her hair back, applied mascara, and put on a rosy pink lipstick. Studying her reflection in the bathroom mirror, she felt frumpy and tired. Yet, it was the best she could do, and deep down, she knew Alan would still appreciate her. After all, he had always reassured her of her beauty.

Straightening her neck, she felt a rush of excitement

pulsing through her. Soon she would see him, and they would be back home together as a family. She wanted to reconnect with him, lay side by side and talk into the night like they used to. Even just to hold one another. Although, she anticipated that his sexual appetite would be heightened after his time on the boat. The prospect of engaging in that kind of intimacy failed to ignite much enthusiasm in her. Nevertheless, she remained determined to make the effort - for Alan's sake. And when she finally saw him, she would allow herself to be swept up in the emotions.

Tammy carefully packed the car, double-checking to ensure she had everything she needed, although she had a nagging feeling that she would likely forget something. Gran stood on the top step, holding Rory tightly in her arms. He was already dozing off again, and Tammy winced, hoping that she might have gotten him to sleep in the pram when she met Alan off the boat. That way, they might have had a few moments to talk. *Never mind.*

Gran gently kissed Rory's head, asking in a whisper while smoothing his back, "Are you sure you have to leave so soon? Couldn't Alan come here for a few days?"

Tammy smiled. "We need to be home together, but thanks Gran."

"Well, I understand," Gran said, observing Tammy's gentle handling of Rory. "I felt the same way when I had your father. You're doing a great job, it's not easy. You're a wonderful mum, Tam." Gran waved from the step, her eyes fixed on them as they drove away.

Tammy drove to the end of the lane, tears welling up in her eyes. She glanced in the rearview mirror, catching sight of Rory's peaceful reflection—he had already fallen asleep. Anger surged within her, her time with Alan would now be cut short. With such a brief nap, Rory was likely to wake up crying and unsettled. Tammy couldn't control anything. She gripped the steering wheel, thinking of Gran's departing words.

Am I a good mum?

Tammy leaned on the pram handle, her gaze fixed on the approaching rusty green boat as it neared the pier. Suddenly, a sharp horn noise pierced the air, startling her and causing Rory to wake abruptly; *it must be Alan behind the wheel.* Distracted by Rory's frantic cries, she swiftly picked him up, attempting to soothe him. Lost in the moment, she failed to notice the boat docking and the men unloading their catch. Alan appeared by her side, playfully pinching her bum. Tammy recoiled inwardly, her attention consumed by Rory's tear-stained face, even as Alan waved goodbye to the other fishermen.

"Come to daddy, son?" Alan reached out for Rory, but Tammy felt a twinge of regret for coming to meet him. Alan smelled of fish, sweat, and dirt, and he wanted to hold her clean, unspoiled Rory. What should she do? She felt helpless. Reluctantly, Rory went to Alan, and Tammy winced as his beautiful white onesie pressed against Alan's dirty overalls. It did little to pacify him; Rory continued crying. Alan handed him back to Tammy, a look of astonishment on his face. "What's wrong with him?"

"He probably needs to be fed again." Tammy steered the pram to the end of the pier, cradling Rory in her arms. Parking the pram beside a paint-peeled bench, she sat down and unbuttoned her blouse.

"What... what are you doing?" Alan gasped, his eyes darting around. "People will see."

Ignoring him, Tammy positioned Rory at her breast. He was hungry. Alan stood in front of her, shielding her from onlookers.

"Tammy, this is not the place - the boys!" He glanced around nervously, saluting another passing fisherman. "Can't we go somewhere else? The car?"

"I'll be done in a minute - the car is quite a walk away! Nobody cares, Alan."

He scoffed, "These guys have been longing for a glimpse of boobs for the past week. Do you really think they won't look?" He moved closer in front of Tammy, his pungent odour invading her nostrils. He muttered something to another passerby.

"Look, why don't you go get the car and come pick us up?" Tammy rummaged in her handbag, her hand failing to find the keys. Panic surged within her. "The keys!" She smacked her forehead with the palm of her hand. "I think I left them in the ignition!"

"You did what?" Alan yelled.

"Just go, please. It's in the car park on the far side," Tammy urged, Rory still nursing at her breast.

"I'm not leaving you here!" Alan protested. "Nobody's going to lay eyes on my wife's..."

"Oh, get over it, Alan - they're just boobs! And your son needs them right now."

"But..."

"Just go."

Tammy exhaled, her eyes fixed on Alan's silhouette storming off the pier toward the main road. This reunion hadn't gone according to plan. She longed for things to go smoothly for once, questioning why everything seemed so chaotic and beyond her control. Glancing down at Rory, she met his blue eyes and let out another breath, gently gliding her finger along his tiny rosy ear. A gentle wind blew, carrying the freshness of the salty air. The fishing boats bobbed on the waves, creating a serene atmosphere. Rory finished feeding, prompting Tammy to sit him upright and gaze at the hazy blue sky above. She thought of her old life when things had been so easy. She yearned to return to work, to be among people, and rediscover her true self. At times, she felt like a mere vessel, with the sole responsibility of feeding Rory. Who was she anymore?

Holding Rory close, she pushed the pram toward the main road, where Alan had parked, his face flushed.

"Thank goodness no one stole it!"

"You're fortunate we live in a place with no crime," Alan remarked, taking charge of the pram and struggling to fit it into the car. Still unfamiliar with most of Rory's accessories, Tammy handed Rory over to him and deftly clicked buttons, neatly organising everything. "Could you take the car home?" Alan smiled, nodding at a man in yellow overalls, crossing the street. "I might stop by for a drink before heading home."

Tammy's heart sank. "But we were supposed to go home together."

"I'll be home soon, Tam. It's been an exhausting week on the boat, and I need some time to unwind."

"But... don't you want to freshen up first? Take a shower?" Tammy grasped at straws, fully aware that once Alan had something in his head, he would be in a foul mood if he couldn't pursue it.

"Nah, look at Don over there. Do you think he's going for a shower?" Alan chuckled, shaking his head.

"Okay," Tammy replied weakly.

"Tell you what, I'll grab a few drinks and come home with something for dinner?" He didn't wait for a response, planting a kiss on Tammy's head before marching determinedly toward the pub.

Tammy stood by the roadside, holding onto Rory. Alan hadn't even offered to help her with putting him in the car seat. His focus was solely on getting drunk, leaving her on her own. She knew his promise of dinner was unlikely, given that he'd probably come home intoxicated, reeking of alcohol and fish. Well, she would make sure she was fast asleep by then. Catching a glimpse of her reflection in the car window, she realised she had hardly spent enough time outside to engage with anyone, let alone have a meaningful conversation. She had hoped that at least Alan would take care of Rory for a while, but she felt like a vessel once again. Tammy stared at her reflection, closing the car door. She was resolved not to waste this opportunity to reclaim her independence and be the fun-loving girl she used to be.

Squinting at Lori's shop at the end of the street, she summoned the strength to go in.

6

R hona spun around in a swivel chair by the front desk and bellowed over the music, "You'll never believe it!"

"You've sold the overpriced outfit in the corner?" Lori peered hopefully, but found the garment still displayed in its usual position.

"No, and it's not overpriced; it's exquisite work, darling!" She said, rolling her eyes. "Anyway...you've won an award!" She beamed, her hands clenched together excitedly in the air. However she soon realised the excitement was all one-sided. "Well?" Rhona rocked on the edge of her chair, her hands retreating to her lap, clutched together.

Lori watched her friend for the punchline to her joke. "Well, what?" She placed down a heavy plastic bag carrying supplements for the shop. Since hiring Rhona, Lori's tea consumption skyrocketed to absurd heights, causing her constant milk shortages and many trips to the bathroom. She rifled through the bag, pulled out a chocolate biscuit and munched on it. "You're pulling my leg." Lori glanced behind Rhona to make sure Tammy wasn't lurking, sniggering at their prank.

"Why would I make up something like that?" Rhona's expression changed to one of outrage.

"I've not entered any competitions. I would know if I won something." Lori sighed, rolling her eyes.

"Well, I'm telling you now!" Rhona groaned. "You know nothing, Ms Robertson, because apparently someone came in here recently and saw what this shop offered."

"Not very much at the moment." Lori chuckled. The fact she couldn't produce enough stock still irritated her. She brushed off the biscuit crumbs from her mouth, and focused her attention back to Rhona. "But hold on... they came here?"

"That's what I'm telling you. You've won... *Most Exciting Business in the Highlands* award," Rhona said, squinting down at her notes.

"That's an award? Never heard of it!"

Rhona rang her hands. "Hey, I will not have this attitude about the business." She coughed, checking herself, then spoke in a softer tone, "What I mean is, lighten up, darling. You are way too hard on yourself. We've got to celebrate these things. If we don't, well...what's the bloody point in doing anything in life?" She sighed, and Lori wondered if her pep talk was about more than the shop.

"You're right," Lori said, biting her lip and smiling at her friend.

"Of course I'm bloody right!" She punched the air with enthusiasm. "This is the beginning, Lori, I can feel it."

Lori grinned at her passion. If she had Rhona by her side, then the business and their friendship would only blossom.

Rhona rubbed her hands together. "Now, I'm dying for a cup of tea. Get the kettle on!"

Rhona placed the newly received glass award on top of the front counter, showing off their success to all who entered the shop. "It adds a certain prestige." She wrinkled her nose, then polished it with her sleeve for the umpteenth time. "Best Business in the Highlands." She sighed.

"*Most Exciting* Business in the Highlands!" Lori laughed, correcting her. Rhona had frequently told their older clients of a far grander award and Lori had no choice but to hold her tongue.

"No one can see the fine print, it's too small on the bottom." Rhona squinted at the engraving. "It really doesn't matter anyway – an award is an award!"

Lori had to agree. Since they'd placed the recent addition on the front counter, more and more people entered, perusing their shelves and rails. As the days rolled on, a constant whirl of customers continued to snap up her latest designs. She rattled through more cutting, stitching and finishing simple tunics in many colours. And as soon as she attached a price tag, shoppers purchased them.

A few days later, Lori was waiting in line at their local store. She looked through the sophisticated Country Chic magazine, only to find her business mentioned in the 'Must Visit' spots in the Highlands. When she showed Rhona the article, her friend snatched the magazine out of her hands, choking on her coffee as she stared at Lori, intermittently reading and rereading the article.

"But this is just amazing!" Rhona coughed, still wheezing from her shock.

Lori's body vibrated with elation. Being featured in a magazine that was exactly aimed at her clientele, without her needing to pay them a penny for the advertisement, was a shock.

"This is priceless!" Rhona jabbed her thumb at the magazine. "So this is why we've had so many people in before the tourist season?"

"Cooey!" Tammy poked her head around the door. "Only me!" She walked in with Rory secured to her chest.

"Oh! Where's the little sausage?" Rhona scurried around the desk and shimmied up to Tammy.

"Shh! He's sleeping!" She beamed, gently patting the bundle.

With a scrunched nose, Rhona made all kinds of shapes with her hands. "But I want a cuddle. He's just so ca-uu-te!" She fawned. "I don't know what it is, even after having three kids, I think I'm done, then I see an ickle-wickle bub and I melt!" She kissed the back of his sleeping head.

"You're broody, Rhona?" Tammy sniggered. "I don't believe it!"

"How can you not be with this wee guy?" She stroked his back, and a small sigh came from within. "Am I right, Lori?" Rhona looked back at Lori, waiting for an answer.

Tammy rocked side to side, patting Rory's bum. "I think that sister of mine is doubtful. She is a successful business-woman, after all." She sat on the chair by the till, her head held high. "Lori, it really is the best thing to happen to me, to us." Tammy sighed dreamily and spun slowly on the swivel chair, keeping the babe in his slumber.

Lori admired Tammy. Her face radiated happiness, being a mum clearly suited her. Unlike other mums covered in spit-up and sporting temporarily greasy hair, Tammy styled her copper locks into an effortlessly messy bun, her lashes were long and her skin flawless. But Lori didn't appreciate the constant jibes. People can surely see that the situation could be complicated – what works for one person might not work for the other. But this was classic Tammy. She knew this by now. If she told Tammy to mind her own business, it would cause a scene – with her sister making Lori feel like the bad guy. No, if she wanted a peaceful life, she must continue to shrug it off, like she'd always done when it concerned Tammy.

Rhona changed the subject quickly, perhaps sensing a sisterly spat, and launched into exciting shop news, listing their latest achievements to Tammy.

"Aw, that's great, Lori, you've worked so hard." Tammy nodded, slightly distracted, stroking Rory's light hair.

"I think it's having Rhona here. She's been my lucky charm."

Rhona clicked her tongue. "I have been told as much by people. I think it's my energy, you know. I've been told I'm psychic too!"

"That's pretty different from being a good luck charm, though!" Lori scoffed, admiring Rhona's undeniable confidence.

Hearing the surrounding commotion, Rory let out a sharp cry, reminding them all of his presence. He moved his head back and forth, unable to get comfortable again and let out another wail.

Rhona gasped, wiggling her fingers, while Lori rolled her eyes at her friend's excitement. Although Lori wanted to help her sister and comfort Rory, she felt like the least experienced person in the room.

Rory's sharp cries continued, and Tammy abruptly stood up, edging to the door.

"Well, some of us have things to do! I better go! See ya later."

Lori watched Tammy bang the door behind her and almost bump into a customer on her departure.

"That was weird." Lori gazed at the door, almost waiting for her sister to reappear. Should she follow her to make sure she was OK?

Rhona greeted their new customer and proceeded to show them the new pieces Lori had made the previous day. Lori smiled politely but soon retreated to her sewing machine, her mind jumbled with thoughts about what she should do. She stretched her neck, regaining focus on her work rather than her sister's behaviour. Lori reassured herself that Tammy, being old enough and opinionated enough, would let her know if something was wrong.

7

Callum packed another box full of used life jackets and stored them at the back of his shed. He had organised his old business equipment by carefully labelling each box. Glancing at his wristwatch, Callum realised his buyer was due any minute; another extreme sports business that was opening on the nearby island. He stacked safety helmets along with head torches and placed them on top of the packed boxes. In between two kayaks, he saw a flowery plastic bag he'd never noticed. Confused, he opened it and found memorabilia from a past he'd hoped to forget. Jennifer's things she must have forgotten to take back with her to New Zealand after their split, or in his blind rage he'd thrown the last of her things in the depths of the shed, hoping to never encounter them again.

Confronting Callum, an old photograph of her stared back at him. In the image, her sun-kissed skin and long blonde hair stood out as she posed atop a nearby hill. Surrounded by a moody landscape, she exuded an air of relaxed confidence, her gaze fixed upon the camera.

Her bright attitude had once held a world of possibilities. She had emanated freshness any young man would want to be around. Callum had called her his 'summer girl'. He scoffed now at the thought – whatever that meant.

He rifled through the bag, not discovering anything too precious: old lip balms, dried-up makeup bottles and post-cards from family in faraway lands. Without thinking, he opened the lid of the lip balm and casually smelled the rosebud fragrance with a burst of strawberry. The scent hit him like a wave and immediately transported him back to New Zealand on that grey day she came into his life.

He had skydived more times than he could count. His grieving over Lori had been all so consuming that he welcomed any distraction. What he didn't expect was to find something more than a distraction in that plane climbing to heights of ten thousand feet. She'd bought the same ticket, another paying customer seeking the thrill of adventure. But her eyes told a different story. Like an innocent deer caught in headlights, she looked over at Callum with growing anguish. Callum's relaxed attitude, having already skydived the previous day in another town, just laughed, as his instructor continually re-checked their buckles and sighed with resignation at their impending doom.

"Oh, dude, I hope you don't trust me with your life?" The German instructor chuckled, unaware he had another spectator who didn't appreciate his jokes and glanced at her own instructor with uncertainty.

Callum shook his head and leaned over the tiny aisle. "I wouldn't listen to this guy. He's won the skydiving champi-onships three years in a row!" The buzz of the plane grew louder, causing him to shout.

Jennifer pressed her lips together in a tight smile. Again, she looked at her own instructor doubtfully.

Callum gritted his teeth. He shouldn't have said

anything. Now the poor girl was going to think her instructor was the least experienced of them all. He leaned back near her once again, closer this time, so he was audible over the plane's vibrations. "Don't worry. These guys are the best in the world. They're all champions. Your guy is the best of them, or so I've heard." Callum nodded back to his German instructor, who was joking with a couple of photographer divers. "My guy won back in the nineties... quite a long time ago, but he's a pro!" Callum winked, and a smile slowly radiated from her. She nodded in silent thanks.

When Callum had landed in a blur of exhilaration, Jennifer immediately marched up to him, buckles and straps trailing behind her, and kissed him there on the field, to wolf whistles. Callum, completely stunned at her forwardness, happily complied.

"You lied about all that stuff about championships, didn't you?" She looked up at him with penetrating light blue eyes.

He shrugged. "There was no point in stressing you out."

She pulled him in again, closer. "I saw you looking at me the whole time on the plane. You're very subtle, aren't you?" She didn't wait for an answer and kissed him again, softer and slower this time, their spectators gradually losing interest and packing up the surrounding equipment.

Callum opened his eyes and placed the lip balm back in the flowery bag along with Jennifer's photograph. She'd been a whirlwind. Even thinking of her now had shaken him upside down, as if he were tumbling in a giant washing machine. It lasted seven years but had felt like a lifetime. A small part of him thought about her now and then, wondering if she was happy. He knew she had a family now back in New Zealand. *A family.* He gritted his teeth, then consciously pushed the old toxic feelings away. He was happy with Lori. The love of his life. He'd always known that, from the first time they met, to last night when they lay together in silence under the covers. He had never fully explained Jennifer's departure to Lori. Even on their adventures away, he knew he needed to explain, but couldn't. He didn't want to taint their time away with his old problems with Jennifer. And there had been so many problems between them; the most obvious being Hector MacDonald. Callum's fists tightened unconsciously. Their affair had done the most damage, making him bitter for years afterwards, almost coming between him and Lori. He would need to tell Lori what happened, properly. All that sorry affair with Jennifer. She deserved to know. But right now, things were good, and he'd do anything to keep them that way.

Craning his neck, he searched for a distraction – another box to pack? He looked at his watch again. The buyer was late.

Callum heard a familiar sound behind him. Interrupting his thoughts was Belinda, the next-door neighbour's cat. She scurried inside the shed, and with no hesitation, frolicked in front of him. Callum bent down to pet her. Whenever he worked in his shed, she would pop her head in, meowing softly. On some occasions, she even ventured up the stairs to his old apartment, sniffing at inanimate objects before settling down on the fluffy rug by his electric fire. Since he and Lori had returned home, he'd spent almost every night at hers, along with her gran and the occasional sleepover from Tammy and little Rory. He smiled thinking of Rory's scrunched-up face. Even at that young age, the little baby's personality was shining through. Callum's mind raced, his thoughts spinning since he started packing up his old life.

He scratched the cat's ear, her white nose moving up and down in ecstasy.

"Who's a good girl? You are, Belinda. I've missed you!" Callum chuckled. The cat purred, dribbling a little at the corner of her mouth. Her owner was the local hairdresser; being a fan of Belinda Carlisle in her youth had prompted the name, which Callum had thought slightly eccentric for a cat, but now, upon reflection, the name actually suited her. Standing up, he looked around at the equipment and various odds and ends he had accumulated over the years.

A part of him wondered if he had been too hasty to end the business. It had been impulsive, even for him. His employee Karen finally used it as her excuse to go back to school, so surely it was meant to be? Nothing lasts forever. Some things need to end to make way for bigger possibilities. He had started *Adventurous Tours* with Jennifer after all, and it was time to start afresh. He had planned to organise his thoughts during his travels with Lori and come up with ideas for his next venture. But that time had been essential in reconnecting with Lori – the last thing he wanted to do was think about work. No, he would be fine. He had worked all his adult life and with savings set aside, he could focus on what mattered.

An outside movement made Belinda quickly dart away, leaving Callum alone, but relieved that the ghosts of his past would soon no longer surround him.

8

Lori scribbled on her notebook, pen in hand, spending the better part of her morning tracking sales for the shop. Gran leaned over the kitchen worktop and placed a large plate of fresh hot scones with satisfaction. The smells of butter and vanilla broke Lori from her trance-like state, and she raised her eyes from her calculations, welcoming a break. However, before pilfering one, she knew better than to succumb to temptation without asking.

"Are you going to a function? It's not the Arlochy Produce Show already?"

Gran had taken part in the community festival every year, displaying her scones, which, in Lori's opinion, were the best she had ever tasted.

"No, these are for here." Gran chuckled. "I just thought my darling granddaughter might like some." She produced a small basket from under the counter and placed a few large fruit scones inside. "Perhaps you could take some with you to the shop today?"

Lori sniffed, placed her pen down, and eyed her grandmother suspiciously. Knowing her gran as well as she did, she could smell a bribe coming.

"Oh, I wondered if you could give me a lift into town later for the community committee meeting?"

Lori cut open a steaming scone, her mouth watering as a large wedge of butter melted over its soft raisins. "Of course, Gran, no problemo." Lori shrugged and went back to her spreadsheet, her senses no longer acute and in much need of repair.

"Oh, and if you could come into the meeting too, that would be lovely." Gran wiped down the already sparkling counter with a well-used tea towel she had got many years ago from Crete. She hummed a tune and nudged the basket of scones next to Lori's elbow.

Lori blinked. "Wait. What? Gran? What are you asking me to do?"

Her gran flicked the dish cloth, her attention fully on it as she folded it slowly. "It's nothing, just a committee meeting tonight in Morvaig. They need to brainstorm fundraising ideas for the area."

Lori inwardly groaned. Morvaig, being the bigger town, hosted most of the events in the area, from which their little village Arlochy benefitted. Her gran was a devoted attendee at every council meeting or local benefit in need of support. Come rain or shine, Mary Robertson would be involved — the first in, sitting at the front, and giving her two cents' worth.

If any townsfolk didn't know her gran, they certainly knew *of* her gran. Her involvement in the community was constant, and even after her stroke, her gran's interest in the committee had grown. But Lori and her gran couldn't have been more different when it came to politics. Lori was happy to sit in the corner and let others bicker amongst themselves, whereas Gran relished the opportunity to give her opinion on any topic.

"Gran, I have the shop. I can absolutely take you anywhere you want to go, that's no problem. But I'm not going into one of those meetings. I'll wait for you in the car, or better yet, you just let me know when it finishes, and I'll come pick you up again." Lori nodded, deciding she would make the most of her time sewing at the shop until she was summoned to act as a taxi for her gran.

Gran chuckled again with a sigh. "Lori, I'm not asking you to sit and watch us. We would like you to come onto the committee board. We need fresh blood, and we decided you're the perfect candidate." After folding and refolding the towel, she placed it by the sink, turning back to Lori.

"Absolutely not! I'm sorry, Gran, I have no time. I have the shop, and even then—"

"Exactly, Lori, you have the shop. You are part of this community now, like it or not. How do you expect to get any support with your shop if you don't show up in the community? Are you serious about your business?"

"Of course I am, but—"

"You're not in New York anymore, my dear. You can't just do your own thing here. If you're getting good business, you must give back. That's how things are done here." Gran's tone had shifted to one of authority, the same she had used when she caught a teenage Lori drinking a can of cider with Rhona by the harbour boat shed.

Lori sighed with irritation. If she didn't do this, she knew it would be worse for her in the long run. She had no choice. She may be a grown woman, but it certainly didn't feel like it sometimes, especially when her gran was concerned. The last thing she wanted was to waste her

Friday night stuck in a stuffy room with even more stuffy people.

Lori looked down at the half-eaten scone and pushed it away. The bribery had worked indeed. "You win, Gran." She sighed again, trying to control her temper.

Gran gave a wink and patted Lori on the cheek. "There's no need to look so glum. It's only a meeting. And there's no winning here, it's just being part of the community." Gran shimmied off, chuckling to herself, Bracken at her heels, leaving Lori pink with rage, her hand clenched around her biro pen.

Lori opened the entrance door of Morvaig Town Hall and stepped into the cold, stale air. Harsh, bright lights greeted her, and she squinted, adjusting her eyes to the echoing hall. Buzzing red heaters blazed on the walls overhead, creating more noise than providing actual heat. In the corner, there was a table with empty cups, saucers, and trays full of sandwiches and cakes. To Lori, it seemed more fitting as a banquet for the local shinty team, rather than the few older committee members who would appear.

A lady, approximately Gran's age, approached them. Lori observed her dark hair pulled back in a loose bun, her glowing tanned skin, and couldn't help but envision her sitting at the head of a large Italian family table. She imagined the woman savouring red wine and laughing into the embrace of warm Mediterranean evenings. It was a stark contrast to the current setting—a draughty hall on a wet Friday in rural Scotland.

"Is it really you, Lori? Your gran speaks about you so often. I remember you as a wee girl, always getting into scrapes!" The woman said warmly in her southern English accent, which had the faintest Scottish hue coming through.

Lori glanced at her gran, who was busy readjusting the baking on the table and fussing over the display, before adding her coveted scones to the assortment. Lori's eyes narrowed as she focused on the scones her gran had initially promised her, now tantalisingly within reach for anyone to snatch.

"I've been meaning to call into your shop, it's just whenever I come into town it's later in the evenings, you know." She nodded, looking Lori up and down. "I must say, you really are like a model from a catwalk." She beamed again.

Lori, embarrassed at the compliment, thanked her graciously but wished for the evening to finish; would she get back to Callum before he turned into bed early? Amidst the recent flurry of achievements and an influx of customers at the shop, Lori had found herself seeing less and less of Callum. Now, with her new committee obligations adding to the mix, those precious moments spent together were becoming even more scarce. She turned her attention back to the woman, unsure of what small talk to indulge in.

"Remember Mrs. Blake?" Gran joined Lori's side, having made no significant adjustments to the baking table, except for the plate of scones, of course.

"Oh, I think Vivian would do, since we are working together." She clasped her hands together.

"Of course!" Lori smiled, recalling Vivian. If there was any function in the area – from school sports days to ceilidh dances – Vivian would be there handing out raffle tickets or prizes to the winners.

"Now, let's start, shall we?" Gran spoke aloud, signalling for the late stragglers to come in and gestured towards the round table on the other side of the hall, the one without cakes. Lori suppressed a laugh, intrigued by her gran's strategy; she just wasn't sure what it was yet.

When they were all seated comfortably, Gran nudged Lori to say a few words. Lori shrugged, unaware she had to make a speech. "Hi, I'm Lori, Mary's granddaughter. I'm here to join the committee?" She pressed her lips together and received murmurs of welcome from the other members. They needed nothing more from her to join the group. And that was OK by Lori.

Gran sighed and rolled her eyes heavenward, seemingly unimpressed or unmoved by Lori's rapid speech. Lori imagined Gran would have prepared a better one herself.

Without another mutter or sideways glance, Gran launched into reading the minutes from the previous meeting. Lori groaned inwardly. She had hoped to never attend another minute-taking meeting for the rest of her life. Ever since she started her career as a buying assistant and was later promoted to a buyer for a prestigious fashion brand, Lori developed a dislike for the meeting culture. The obligatory meetings often resulted in delays in everyone's individual work and burdened them with additional tasks after each session. An important factor in why Lori adored running her own business—no more enforced meetings!

Lori made an attempt to tune in to the committee's recent plans, but her mind drifted, reflecting instead on Gran's unwavering dedication to the area. It was truly admirable. Earlier that evening, as they drove to the hall, Mary had unleashed a passionate speech about how these meetings held the power to transform their area into the ultimate paradise. Picture more tourists, thriving businesses, top-notch schools, and leisure facilities that would make heads spin! But as Lori glanced around the table, she couldn't help but notice the worn-out expressions on the faces of her fellow attendees. It was far from the enchanting King Arthur scene her gran had painted. To Lori's amusement, two older gentlemen seated beside her seemed more interested in ogling the buffet table at the far end of the hall than listening to the minutes. Clearly, their motivation for attending these gatherings didn't involve a desire for a better swimming pool!

Gran finished listing the previous week's minutes, and before Lori could look forward to a scone, Vivian spoke spiritedly of tedious topics such as parking spaces and the annual traditional music festival.

Lori couldn't blame the two men beside her, she soon daydreamed of other things, too. Things that held more interest than mundane council matters. Lori's expression glazed over as she watched Vivian and her gran exchanging ideas, her mind secretly filling with images of Callum's strong arms, recalling the night he lifted her up. She soon fell into a dream-like state and wondered if she got home early enough... might he lift her again? This time shirtless or maybe in the shower? Just as Lori became fully distracted by Callum's bare chest, the entrance door slammed, snapping her out of her daydream, and a very tall man, slightly stooped, strode in with a folder under his arm. Lori's grandmother groaned quietly beside her and massaged her temple with her right hand. Vivian turned back to them, eyebrows raised, while the few remaining members made their own shuffles and grunts. Unsure what was happening, Lori examined the man who approached them. He was older too, his face tinged with grey and set deep in his head were light eyes that penetrated the room like an eagle.

"You started early?" He pointed an accusatory finger in their direction.

Gran stood up slowly. "Mr Green, I can assure you we

didn't start early. If anything, we're a little late tonight." Gran enunciated her words clearly, her Highland accent slightly changing.

"It said eight in the paper." His finger pointed to the ground, in an aggressive manner.

Impulsively, Lori stood up. But before she could intervene, her gran smiled and shook her head slightly. "This is my granddaughter, she has joined the committee, and we're all delighted to have fresh ideas that will hopefully benefit the area." Gran patted Lori's shoulder gently, making her slowly sit down.

"I see, another Robertson on the committee. I'm sure you would like the whole family here, so you can push your own agenda on the community."

Lori, gobsmacked, raised her chin to find her gran composed and radiating in calm poise.

"Well, Mr Green, that is simply untrue. We need more people on the committee, as you are fully aware, since we have asked you to join on many occasions."

"You lot need watched. I wouldn't join the committee if it paid me." He pulled out a nearby chair, next to the cake display, which made one of the other gentlemen slightly jumpy. Mr Green crossed his legs, folded his arms and placed the ring binder on his lap.

"Mr Green, we volunteer to help the community, not disrupt its improvements." Gran sat down, her face turned away from Mr Green's general direction, and continued discussing parking spaces, ignoring the frosty atmosphere lurking in the far corner.

Since Lori was new, they requested she take the minutes to familiarise herself with the tasks to be done. She obliged, but her mind still fizzed with distractions – not Callum's arms this time, but the unfriendly man with fierce eyes.

Lori had been away from her old job for some time. The environment had been stressful, but she hadn't encountered anything like this in their meetings. Sure, there would be disagreements and objections, but never anything so hostile. There was more politics at play here than they made out, she was sure of it. Unable to kill her curiosity, she stole a glance at Mr Green; he kept his eyes down, as if concentrating on listening more than watching, then with sudden energy, jotted down notes. Lori wondered if he was taking his own minutes, but then quickly adjusted her attention back to the meeting. Luckily, no one had noticed her lack of interest in committee business, but she would need to write something soon. She glanced back at Mr Green's dipped head and considered asking him for his notes at the end of the meeting. Perhaps not, she reconsidered. Her gran would surely disown her on the spot.

Oh, how she hated small-town politics.

After what felt like six hours of committee business, Lori sighed as she finally arrived home and quietly let herself into her bedroom. The curtains were open, allowing the moon to shine over Callum's silhouette on the bed. Lori took off her clothes and let down her curls, massaging her scalp briefly after having her hair tied up all day. Crawling into bed, she kissed the back of Callum's neck and ear, stroking his bare shoulder. She wanted his weight on top of her. It had felt like forever since those delicious nights on the beach in Vietnam.

"Darling, I'm home. Come and warm me up," she whispered in his ear.

A sudden snore sounded and he rolled over onto his stomach, lost in a deep sleep.

Lori exhaled with disappointment and remained on her side. The full moon peaked from behind the clouds, his smirk showing again. *Why was he always smirking like that?* She shut her eyes, pushing away distracting thoughts that wanted to come calling. She considered waking Callum; a gentle nudge to talk about his day. No, that wouldn't be fair. He was as busy as she was. If Lori wanted to talk, she'd need to make more of an effort. And she would.

Lori turned away from Callum to let him rest – but mainly to avoid the moon's smugness – and tried resolutely to get some sleep.

9

J ean's frustration surged within her, her arms crossing tightly in an attempt to contain her mounting fury. "It's not just my time you're wasting," she seethed. "You're wasting your own!"

Her students, relentless in testing her patience, whispered among themselves, their disregard a constant thorn in her side. A pang of irritation struck her as she noticed some of them sneaking glances at their phones. Their phones! How had she lost such control over her once orderly class?

The calm, disappointed approach had been ineffective, and Jean knew she needed to shift tactics. Inhaling deeply, she gathered her resolve. "Listen up!" she bellowed, causing a few startled giggles from the girls in the front row. "Don't you all want to pass your exams?"

Yet again, they ignored her words, and soon the mutterings started up again.. Determination surged through her. "Silence!" Jean's voice sliced through the air, but the chatter persisted. Flushing with frustration, she pressed on. "I can see that learning is the last thing on your minds," she pleaded, desperation lacing her words. "But if not education, then what? Failing your exams? Embarking on a life of mediocrity? Getting pregnant before you're ready? Settling for a job that drains your soul? Is that what you want?" *Nothing.* The edge of her ruler crashed against the front desk. "I don't know why I bother!" Jean's voice shrieked with anger. "Most of you will end up in prison anyway!" The words erupted from her.

A heavy silence fell upon the classroom. Every eye on her.

Rubbing her weary head, Jean sighed. Each day seemed to transform into a battle she inevitably lost. She turned her gaze back to the whiteboard, where she had painstakingly dissected the main themes of Shakespeare's Hamlet, an endeavour she had undertaken alone as her class paid little attention. How could she reel them back in? Was it her shortcomings or their collective indifference to blame? Before Jean could muster the energy for further contemplation, a familiar face appeared at the door, peering through the window, beckoning her.

Karen's arrival stirred a spark of concern within Jean. "Is everything alright? Is it the girls?" Her mind instantly veered toward the negative. She hadn't looked at her phone all morning.

Karen held up a paper bag with a warm smile. "No, I just thought I'd surprise you with lunch," she said, her voice filled with an air of excitement. "Um, hello?" Karen waved to the now quiet class behind Jean, their eyes intently fixed on her.

"It's not lunch for another hour," Jean muttered through clenched teeth, this interruption being the last thing she needed.

Karen's expression faltered. "Oh, sorry. I thought..." She shook her head, her blonde hair swishing gently. "Nevermind, I could wait here until you're done," she suggested, a hopeful grin playing upon her lips.

Suddenly, a voice from the back of the class broke the silence. "Who's this, Miss?" One boy called out.

Jean's mind raced, searching for the appropriate response. "Never you mind!" she snapped, attempting to deflect the inquiry.

"Is this your girlfriend?" Another student chimed in.

Jean froze, caught off guard. What should she say? Her gaze darted to Karen, who awaited an introduction. "This is Karen," Jean uttered, hoping to ward off any further teasing. "My friend." she quickly added, before Karen could interject.

Jean longed for a shower as the school bell rang, feeling sticky and drained. The day seemed endless. She ventured out into the fresh air, squinting in the bright light. She spotted Karen by the stream that ran behind the school grounds, sitting on her jacket, her hair swept up, and her arms bared in a white tank top. Rolling up the cuffs of her jeans, she soaked up the sun.

"Well, isn't this lovely?" Jean plopped down beside Karen, careful to avoid the damp grass.

"It's turned into such a beautiful day," Karen sighed. "Cheese or ham?" She presented two rolls.

Jean grabbed the nearest one and bit into it eagerly, washing it down with a bottle of orange juice Karen had magically produced. She munched on a handful of salty crisps.

"Are you hungry?" Karen chuckled.

"Starving!" Jean replied, her mouth full.

"You didn't have breakfast?"

Jean shook her head. "No time. I was running late today because I had to drop the girls off for their swimming lesson."

Karen frowned. "Jean, you should have asked me to take them."

"But you have your studies."

"Yeah, but I can manage these things, too. I have the time."

Jean disliked asking for favours. It always left her feeling obligated to return the gesture.

"Maybe I should spend more mornings with you guys?" Karen suggested cheerfully, slipping on a pair of sunglasses from her small backpack. "I could even make breakfast for you all, and then you can eat while I take the girls to their early sessions."

"That's a big ask," Jean murmured, her appetite fading. "You already have so much on your plate."

"My exams aren't until later, and I love spending time with you." Karen affectionately touched Jean's shoulder and then moved her hand toward the nape of her neck. Usually, this gesture led to a kiss on Jean's neck or lips. Jean looked around. Thankfully, they were alone, except for a couple of younger students playing with a ball in the distance.

Jean leaned into Karen's touch, yearning for a kiss but wary of the risk of getting caught. Karen's hazel eyes sparkled as they locked onto Jean's. Her kindness enveloped Jean like a warm embrace, and for a moment, everything else faded away. Jean reached for Karen's hand and squeezed it. "Only if you're sure. I don't want to take advantage," Jean said, her mind already contemplating what she might have to do for Karen in return.

Karen inched closer, her breath grazing Jean's arm. With

a mischievous smile, she whispered in Jean's ear, "Maybe you could take advantage of me later?"

Jean desired her intensely. All other thoughts vanished into the distance. One last glance around to ensure no prying eyes, and with newfound confidence, she pulled Karen close, their lips meeting in a passionate kiss. Their tongues danced playfully.

"That would be my pleasure," Jean murmured, feeling the weight of the day finally lifting from her shoulders.

10

E ach morning, Lori woke earlier than the previous day. The brightness of a new dawn sparkled across the west coast, bringing them all into spring with a gentle nudge. With Tammy staying another few nights in her old room, Lori was up most of the night, disturbed by Rory's rather loud demands for milk.

She pulled on her running shoes, zipped up her fleece jacket and put on a vintage baseball cap to hide her unruly morning curls. Her bleary-eyed sister, who insisted she didn't need help and would be perfectly capable of taking Rory out in due course, obstructed Lori from taking her nephew out. Her attempts fell on deaf ears, as Lori determinedly fixed the baby in his carrier, buckling him in close to her chest, the process of which came easily to her after watching a stream of 'how to' videos on YouTube in the early hours. Popping on his woolly hat to cover his pink ears, she threw a long shawl over them both, shielding him from any chilly wind. Tammy sighed resignedly and with a weak wave, closed her bedroom door.

The morning haar skimmed the sea, concealing the red

and blue fishing boats anchored along the shoreline. Lori breathed in deeply and glanced down at Rory, whose manner had calmed immediately when they both stepped into the cool air. He gazed up at her, his almond blue eyes watching her intently with a quiet interrogation that made Lori laugh aloud.

"You are a suspicious Robertson indeed." She chuckled to the bundle and ventured off in search of coffee.

Her local cafe along the main street came into view; a bright yellow terraced building squeezed in between the library and local craft shop. Its yellow theme continued in the hanging flowers at the doorway and in various pots clustered around the windows and along its white wall. A small hatch at the side welcomed takeaway orders – a busy spot for locals needing a coffee on the go and their daily gossip allowance refilled. Luckily for Lori, today, she was the only one.

She perused the menu, debating whether to bring some vanilla tarts back to Gran's, until the hatch window slid open and a face popped out, taking Lori by surprise.

"If it isn't Lori Macnori?" called the familiar blonde.

Francesca.

Francesca smiled broadly, exposing natural white teeth like an American actress, although the smile looked more genuine than Lori believed. Leaning an elbow on the ledge casually, her inquisitive hazel eyes scanned the baby fastened to Lori, but she said nothing.

Lori was stunned by her serene manner and couldn't think of anything to say, especially since she hadn't seen Francesca working in the cafe before. Now she was in Lori's village, Arlochy. *Great!* Until now they had enjoyed the short distance apart, with Francesca living on the outskirts of Morvaig. Meaning their paths rarely crossed. But if she was going to be in Lori's domain, a new coffee shop would need to be found... a tough thing to find when it was the only cafe in her village.

A sharp fart noise erupted from Rory, and Francesca chuckled to herself. Lori patted his bum, making it obvious it was the baby who farted and not her. Francesca's breezy manner still affected Lori. Had it never occurred to her that all those years ago in high school, she'd made Lori miserable? Lori shook off the tightening sensation around her shoulders and had to switch off that part in her mind before it dragged her back to her awkward teen years.

Nope, too late.

Lori's hands clenched at her sides. She couldn't shake the gut feeling that her nickname, Lori Macnori, had been invented by Francesca. A nickname that followed her throughout high school. One that seemed harmless, and many called her it, without really knowing its origin.

Callum being one of them.

The unfortunate event that inspired the name was a special lunchtime of sushi. Their school had celebrated different cultures from around the world, and whether it had been from the sushi or something else, Lori vomited all down her front, right there in the cafeteria. Running to the safety of the girl's toilets, she'd scrubbed her school uniform, but to no avail. Rhona had comforted her in the girl's toilets, rubbing her back, reassuring her that everyone would soon forget about the incident. As mortified as Lori was, she clung to the hope that Rhona was right, that it would pass from everyone's recollection.

She persevered, ignoring the jibes and rowdy boys who pretended to vomit whenever she passed. Over time, it became less spoken of, and just when she thought she had escaped the humiliation, the nickname surfaced and she was right back in that cafeteria every time she heard it.

Francesca's long blonde hair was loosely pulled into a ponytail to show off her long neck, her silk white shirt unbuttoned to show a sliver of cleavage; she was effortlessly beautiful, and Lori felt deflated. She had never been that insecure about her own appearance, even after years of working with the most beautiful women in the world. From Costner's marketing campaigns to attending fashion shows, her career had exposed her to the world of models. Their looks not easily replicated with a bit of lipstick or mascara.

But something about Francesca made her question herself.

They shared a layered history. No matter how much Lori tried to cover it up, it was there. Like a giant pimple she could never conceal. The pimple, so to speak, was Francesca's friendship with Callum. They had been close long before Lori and Callum were reunited. But even though he insisted nothing had ever happened with Francesca, as much as she trusted him, she did not trust Francesca.

Callum had frequently asked Lori to make an effort with his old friend, but with their unpleasant history, she just couldn't bring herself to. But now there was no hiding – Francesca was in front of her and she couldn't run away as much as she desperately wanted to.

"Hi, Francesca." Lori smiled, rubbing Rory's back, hoping he'd done as much farting as he was going to.

"You caught me by surprise there. I didn't think you had a baby?"

"No, he's my sister's. Tammy's."

"Yeah, that sounds about right. I'd have thought Callum would have said something, of course, unless it was some other man's child!" She giggled. "Naughty! But yes, this is Tammy and Alan's squige?"

Lori recoiled inside. "Aye."

"I know Alan. He plays shinty with Callum, of course! I've met him a few times. Boy, he can party hard, that one, especially after they've won a match!" Francesca shook her head, her ponytail lightly flicking from side to side.

Lori hadn't realised her old nemesis still met up with Callum, and now, apparently, Alan! As much as she wanted to be perfectly calm, she couldn't help but feel hurt to think Callum was quietly leading a second life, partying in the local pubs after their matches, with Francesca hanging off him. Did he really think that was acceptable way to behave?

He'd seemed a little distracted of late. Maybe he was out celebrating some game or another. Lori had to admit, she had lost track of what he may or may not be doing. But even if she temporarily lost a little interest in what shinty matches he was playing, that didn't make it OK for him to be socialising with Francesca on the sly. No matter how Lori felt about Callum and their relationship, she couldn't shake the feeling that something had happened between them, at least before Lori came back from New York.

She needed to find out. She needed to know.

Lori gladly gave her coffee order in between Francesca's description of her exceptional skills as a barista and how everyone from the nearby islands would call in for her roast in particular.

"You tell Callum to call me. I need some help with my washing machine." She nodded, handing a large paper cup through the hatch.

Lori smiled again, teeth clenched. *I bet you need something fixed.* Outraged that her boyfriend was called upon to act as maintenance man for a girl who had been pampered all her life.

Lori knew she had to calm down, to stop being so serious, that Francesca was just a product of her surroundings – she knew no better. But why couldn't she call a professional like everyone else?

Lori walked onwards towards the end of the village and up a dirt track. The motivation from earlier slipping through her fingers as she traipsed slowly uphill. Rory remained still, his eyes now flickering, falling into sleep. Lori made it to the scenic lookout at the top of the hill where tall pine trees towered over a wooden bench. She squinted at the it, running her hand along its grooves until she found it: her and Callum's initials. They were still there, a little faint with time, but remained etched in the wood. She sat down, looking out towards the sea over a canopy of trees. The fresh pine fragrance surrounded her and lulled Rory into an even deeper sleep. She leaned forward and sipped the coffee.

Francesca was right – she did make excellent coffee.

Lori stayed quiet in the stillness, hearing only a squawking bird in the distance, with more gentle noises coming from Rory snuggled against her. Wilfully adjusting her mindset, she listed all the things in her life to be grateful for, or she *should* be grateful for. She had a successful business, a loving boyfriend and family all around her. That much was true. But why did an uneasy feeling niggle at her?

Just like the evenings before high school, she lay awake, anxiously expecting to be teased the next day. But no matter what convincing excuses she gave to Gran; she would be on the school bus the next morning without fail. She felt like she was always going to be that vomiting girl from high school. Was this what lay underneath it all? After months of travelling, years living and working in another country, was one glimpse of her old bully from school going to derail her and cause everything she worked hard to achieve, to disappear in a blink of an eye?

Lori stroked Rory's back as shards of yellow light dowsed the landscape. She kept still, taking in the view for some moments. An icy wind picked up, making her shiver.

She drained the last of her coffee and was about to stand until she saw a rare sight. Creeping down a tree trunk, a red squirrel scurried down to the bottom, stopping several times to check over his shoulder for predators. Lori held her breath as it flicked its tail and darted towards a cluster of white flowers covering the hill directly in front of her. The creature swiftly weaved in and out between the petals, licking and tasting some sweet nectar, and as quickly as Lori adjusted her gaze to the scene, the little fellow scurried up the same tree trunk out of view.

Rory's eyes blinked open, gazing at her with his usual suspicious look. If Lori didn't know better, she would have believed the red squirrel was a sign, but what kind of sign? She picked up the empty coffee cup and slowly made her way back down the hill, leaving her thoughts on the wooden bench.

11

L ori adjusted her fitted orange cardigan and ran her fingers through her smooth hair. She had attempted teasing her frizz with a straightening iron at work, and so far her hair had behaved... although each second she stayed outside, the volume seemed to expand. With a birthday present for Tammy in one hand and a bottle of wine for dinner in the other, she tapped on the door.

It burst open and her two nieces erupted in a chorus of 'Happy Birthday'.

"It's me!" Lori whispered, stepping into the brightly lit hallway.

"You look like Auntie Tam!" Anne's widened eyes scanned Lori's hairstyle.

"Really?" Lori had always felt incredibly different to both her sisters, but had to admit that their similarities became more apparent the more time they spent together. "Well, we are sisters." She nodded in agreement, taking the compliment of looking like her younger sister.

Lori squeezed her nieces tightly and followed them to Jean's kitchen. Her older sister welcomed her by placing a large glass of red wine into her hand and shooing her girls to set the table. Jean had various pots going on the stove, some bubbling gently, others more aggressively. Her face flushed as she pulled off a pot that bubbled over, her usual calm composure disappearing momentarily as she turned on the noisy fan above the oven, wafting a towel to disperse any steam and smoke.

"Can I help?" Lori offered, awkwardly sipping her wine as her sister flustered.

"No no, you relax!" She placed a bowl and chopping board on the counter, then cut into two avocados. She turned back to the stove and swore under her breath as the same pot began to bubble over again. "This bloody rice won't ever cook!" She fumed, and Lori shimmied around the counter to deal with the avocados, taking the pressure off Jean to make the guacamole.

"It's all good, Jean, it's only us. We don't need anything fancy. And Tammy loves your cooking." Her tone was soft, but her reassurances had little effect on Jean.

Jean's eyes darted all around and she leaned against the sink, the tea towel still in her hand. "It's not that... I..." She shook her head. "I just shouldn't have had a dinner tonight. What was I thinking! I didn't want Gran to cook. She's still recovering and shouldn't need to plan a party, but now it's the last thing I want."

Lori stopped mashing the avocados and met her sister's eyes. "How? What's happened?"

"It's fine," she whispered, watching the door, then edging towards it to peer into the next room where Maggie and Anne were watching tv. The dinner table was already set with napkins, glasses, and a few large candelabras by the large bay windows.

Jean's house perched atop a picturesque hill, over-looking Morvaig town and the bustling ferry harbour. As the evening sun dipped behind the rolling hills, a golden hue enveloped the landscape, creating an ambient setting. Yet down below, the streetlights flickered to life, casting a glow on the streets adorned with an array of restaurants and pubs. The air was filled with anticipation as the tourist season began, and the lively coastal town buzzed with energy.

Jean gently closed the kitchen door behind her and unscrewed the bottle of wine, pouring its contents into an empty glass. She leaned against the sink, her hand wrapped around the glass stem, her mind clearly somewhere else. "Things are confusing. Karen and I have been really great, but things are still new. She mentioned the other day about house hunting, and she's found a nice place, further along the coast, and says it would be perfect for us all." Jean frowned and bit her lip. "I should be happy, but it's too soon. The girls!" She stopped and bit her lip again. "They are still too young and don't understand. They think Karen is a friend... Everyone thinks Karen is a friend!"

"Well, we don't. We know you're more than that."

Jean shrugged. "But they don't. They're too young. I will tell them... but-but," she stuttered, her eyes glistening, then shook her head. "I shouldn't be thinking this, especially tonight. I wanted everyone to have a nice evening. Gran, Tammy and you – you all have so much on your plates!"

Lori's heart ached for her sister and she wanted to hug her but knew the action would leave them both in floods of tears.

Jean gulped her wine. A tear trickled down her cheek, she wiped it away angrily.

Lori squeezed her sister's shoulder briefly. "OK, what we're going to do is finish this dinner – you've done almost everything. I just need to put the tortillas in the oven and we'll dish out the food when they arrive. Just take a breath, Jean, things will work out. Tomorrow, things might look different."

Jean nodded, breathing out slowly. "You're right, Lo."

"Cooey!" Gran popped her head around the kitchen door.

"We better get this food dished out then!" Lori sighed with a smile. "Hi, Gran."

"This is where all the action is. What have I missed? My girls in here gassing away without me." Gran joked, wrapped in a deep green scarf over a velvet dress with jewel-like shapes of rich purple, pinks and jade. She scanned Jean's face, and a look of concern fell across her features. "Has something happened?"

"No, Gran, Jean just cut her finger, but she's better now, right?" Lori encouraged her big sister's reaction to her impromptu story.

"Oh, Jeany, is there anything I can do?" Gran placed down a package wrapped in flowery pink paper, with a large white bow on top. She took off her scarf, making herself ready for work.

"Absolutely not, Gran, I want you to relax tonight. No jobs, apart from spending time with Maggie and Anne." Jean smiled and began pulling out dishes.

Gran chuckled. "Well, that's not a job, that's my pleasure." She accepted a glass of wine from Lori and went through to sit beside her great-granddaughters.

Once everyone devoured the meal, Tammy propped herself on the couch and nursed Rory while Lori refilled everyone's glasses.

"Thanks for the meal, Jean, it was delicious." Tammy cradled Rory in the nook of her arm and glanced back to the rest of the women who remained by the dining table.

Gran clasped her hands and looked at the view; spots of light illuminated the bay, showing the fishing boats heading out for their nightly voyage. "How's Alan?" She said aloud over the tv. Maggie and Anne lay on the floor, their attention engrossed in some children's show featuring a giant blue puppet.

"Girls, please!" Jean raised her eyebrows, the gesture more than enough for Anne to understand and speedily turn the volume down.

"He's good. He's just been so busy. His last trip home was so brief, but he's home next week for some extra time... although he mentioned there were some upcoming shinty matches on his time off. Not exactly what I wanted to hear, but I can imagine Lori's got the same issue with Callum?"

Distracted, Lori had been engrossed in her thoughts, contemplating the design of a ball gown. Her gran's jewel-coloured dress had given her the idea of a new style using art deco shapes. She'd decided on the colour of fabric and the shape around the neckline, but still needed to sketch out her thoughts. If she could get a pad of paper from her nieces, perhaps she could get the bones of a design before the evening was out.

"Lori?" Tammy creaked her head back.

"Hmmm?"

"Yes, where is Callum tonight? He's been hiding the last few days." Gran remarked. "I even had his favourite rhubarb crumble sitting in the fridge, and what did I find? None of it eaten!"

"That's awful, Gran, you must be losing your touch." Jean giggled, her previous upset vanished.

"He's been sorting out his house, and yeah, Tammy, he's told me about the matches. He says they're going on a mini tour around the Highlands... again. I expect they'll be gone for a week."

"These bloody shinty matches. Sometimes I feel he prioritises hitting a ball with a stick over spending time with his wife and child!" Tammy shook her head vigorously, her swearing making Gran flinch.

Lori had left out the tiny but important detail that Callum had asked her to go with him and explore the northern Highlands together. But she was struggling so much to keep the shop stocked that she couldn't afford the time off. After their discussion, he had stayed at his flat to "organise" his things, but Lori knew he was secretly angry and didn't want to admit it.

Well, *she* was angry. She had seen Francesca *three* times in the last two days, through no fault of her own. Each time Francesca confronted her with smugness and over familiar comments about Callum, that made Lori bristle like a cat stroked the wrong way.

"You marry the man, you marry his job!" Jean gritted her teeth and shrugged her shoulders.

"It's not his job though!" Tammy's voice boomed over the tv. Maggie and Anne gawped at her. "I mean," she lowered her voice, "they don't even get paid. They may get expenses paid, but really it's just a hobby. If he was getting money, that would be different, but leaving his family just so he can play a bloody match!" Tammy's face flushed, and she looked down at Rory who was still nursing, gazing at her.

Lori noticed Gran wince again, most likely at all the "bloodys" Tammy uttered. The atmosphere had turned chilly, and it was becoming increasingly apparent that Tammy and Alan were not coping well after all.

Tammy sniffed gently and wiped her eye. "I'm sorry, I'm fine. It's just the hormones. I need to sleep, that's all. Hopefully, this wee lad will give me some rest tonight." She raised Rory from the crook of her arm and burped him.

"What can we do, Tam?" Gran got up slowly and moved towards her granddaughter, then perched on the couch by her side. "I'm here to help."

Tammy patted her gran's hand fondly. "You don't need to do anything, Gran. Rory needs me, and I just need to go with the flow. We'll be alright. I just look forward to Alan coming home...again!"

Gran tenderly scooped up Rory, holding him close in her embrace. The little one was so content and satisfied from his feeding that he quickly drifted off into a peaceful slumber.

Lori's gaze lingered on the twinkling lights below as she searched for Callum's house within the cluster. Should she go to him tonight? Was he thinking of her now, or maybe he was preparing his things before leaving for the match? Lori wondered how all three sisters' problems had come to the surface tonight, like they were in sync with one another. Like a dance, at first swaying in time, but now all falling down together. Things would surely look up. They would go back to how things were. It was only temporary. Things had to get better.

Lori dragged her attention from the glowing yellow

lights outside and back to the candlelight before her. They spent the rest of the evening eating cake and taking it in turns to wash dishes. As the evening crept later, Lori made a decision to let sleeping dogs lie and chose not to go to Callum after all.

12

"Tell me more!" Rhona bent over the cutting table, entranced. Her perfectly drawn cat-eye makeup made her blue eyes look even more intense as she listened to every detail of Lori's committee meeting escapades. Lori may have embellished a little more for entertainment value, but Gran's head-to-head with Mr Green had amplified since their last meeting.

Lori hadn't expected another visit from Mr Green, but the tall, imposing man made his position known on all matters, which led to a somewhat heated debate with her gran over their upcoming Highland games.

"We discussed this several months ago, Mr Green. I believe you were holidaying in…" Gran paused.

"Malta!" Mrs Blake nodded in solidarity with Gran, the two ladies enjoying their teamwork in bringing down Mr Green bit by bit.

Gran raised her eyebrow. "Our committee meetings are apparently not so important, compared to a sun lounger and a good book, I don't doubt." She pressed her lips tightly. "Although I was astounded to see you come back paler than when you left. Perhaps you were indoors, Mr Green? Did you interfere with their community matters over there too?" Gran batted her eyelashes, causing a flustered and confused Mr Green to retreat to his seat.

"One point to your gran," Rhona hooted, licking her finger and swiping the air. "If I didn't know better, I'd say she was enjoying the rivalry."

Lori had to agree. After the meeting, her gran certainly appeared to have a spring in her step.

"That's because she's getting in the last word, but he's relentless, Rhona! I just worry about her health. This angry man can't be helping." Lori frowned. She'd been rearranging a terracotta scarf around a mannequin neck for the last ten minutes, her mind absent from the task at hand.

"Your gran has spirit, but she isn't a silly woman... if she doesn't feel well, she'll tell you."

Lori wished Rhona was right, but her gran was a determined soul through and through – she would fight until her last breath. Even after Gran's reassurances about getting better after the stroke, Lori found she just couldn't fully relax. Each day she made several phone calls to Gran, as well as asking Callum to double-check on her (when they were talking, that is!). Lori's stomach did a strange lurch thinking of Callum. She had said goodbye to him earlier that morning as he stepped onto the bus with the shinty team, his face showing little emotion. They hadn't really spoken properly about her not going with him, but she couldn't leave the shop. She may have Rhona there, but she could hardly expect her friend to sell the negligible number of garments they had. Lori needed to be there, creating more products and generating more profit. She couldn't pause things to follow Callum around the Highlands like a lovesick shinty groupie or WAG!

Frustrated, she tied a loose knot in the scarf and anxiously wrung her hands, giving the mannequin an irritated push.

"Everything OK?" Rhona squinted suspiciously, but a fisherman sauntering past the window momentarily distracted her and she waved. He looked at the window display and with a tilt of his head, saluted Rhona.

"Is there anyone you don't know?" Lori changed the subject, watching the retreating fisherman. His stained yellow waterproofs and blue woolly beanie hat made her stop a moment to imagine those colours in an outfit. "Swing skirt... with a buttoned blouse," she murmured to herself and pressed up against the window to get the last glimpse of the figure before he turned the street corner. Feeling around the cutting table for a pen before the image left her mind completely, she sketched a silhouette.

"Eh? That was Don, you know Don? Old Donald MacIntyre from up Blar Hill over on the far side of Morvaig."

Lori nodded, intending to give the impression that she was well aware of who and what Rhona was referring to.

She didn't.

Lori knew far fewer people than Rhona did and had hoped she would have got better on her return home.

She hadn't.

Lori couldn't remember all the place names. Even though she had grown up in the area, she remained slightly mortified at what she believed she should know. On this occasion, she believed Blar Hill might have been in Morvaig or perhaps on the outer village further south. It was all so very confusing, but having Rhona around may prove handier than she first thought.

"Anyway," Rhona leaned back on the cutting table, "is everything OK? You seem a bit agitated."

"I'm good. Great, really." Lori nodded, but her friend's look pressed her for more. She sighed and pushed aside her sketch. "I think I need help."

"I could've told you that ages ago, honey!" Rhona scoffed but retracted as soon as Lori flashed one of her own hard looks.

"I mean, I need help around the shop."

"But I'm here!" Rhona's mouth opened in confusion.

"I mean *more* help. We're struggling a bit. Not with sales exactly, but we need more product to sell."

Rhona tapped her chin, considering the dilemma. "I wish I could sew. It's just not my thing... I can't even sew a button on my kids' clothes. Malcolm does all those jobs!"

"Really?" Lori couldn't imagine Malcolm sewing. As a cow farmer, he gave the impression of being traditional. A large man with hands like shovels – Lori imagined the extra effort it took him to hold a tiny needle without fumbling. "Malcolm is a multi-talented fella. Maybe I should have asked *him* to help in the shop!"

"Hey!" Rhona snapped.

"Joking! Hey, Rhonz, it's fine, you're doing loads. It's just something Callum said today before he got on the bus."

Rhona's quizzing expression didn't tap Lori for further information. Instead, Lori pulled the sketch back towards her. The folds of the skirt would need a lot of fabric to achieve such a silhouette, but the tiny buttons up the front bodice of the shirt gave a sophisticated yet dramatic look. She was sure if she combined the colours she'd seen the fisherman wearing, it would carry off the style beautifully.

Rhona followed Lori's scrutinising eye. "That's pretty fabulous, Lo. Did you just come up with that?" She placed her fingers on the scrap paper, following the lines of the skirt. "You're getting so bloody good at this. It's like you're meant to do this. I can't believe you didn't sew all those years abroad!"

Lori's travels prior to coming back home for good composed of Australia and New York, where she gained a vast amount of experience in fashion, but on the corporate side of things. In high school she had an interest, following in her mother's footsteps, who had her own box of patterns she would alter and reproduce designs for her daughters. Since her mother's passing all those many years ago, it had been Lori who remained interested, and when she opened the shop, her confidence in designing and sewing blossomed.

"It's just pouring out of me at the moment." Lori dragged her gaze from the sketch to the photo of her mother on the wall.

Abruptly, Rhona hit the table with such force it broke Lori out of her melancholy daydream. "I've got it! I know what you should do…about the shop, I mean!" Rhona could barely contain her excitement. "OK, you've not got loads of stock to fully fill this place. Well, that's fine, what we do is stock other designers' work!"

Lori screwed up her nose.

"Wait! Just hear me out." Rhona pointed her finger accusingly, then took a moment to process her thoughts before nodding. "You don't have to stock their work forever, you could say you're giving them a trial-run for the summer… that means the pressure is not completely on you to have work here. Of course, you'll have the shop with your designs but the other pieces can be accessories, things that can enhance what we already have, then we don't need to worry about empty rails in the shop."

With a quick glance, Lori surveyed the shop. Even if she

jam-packed the place with her work, there would still be room for hats, scarves and jewellery.

Her initial intention of opening a shop was to create and sell directly to the public, bypassing the bureaucratic nature of the fashion industry. It would serve as her creative outlet, with the added hope of making money. But if she could help others, and maybe the pieces could complement one another, giving as much value to the customer as possible, then wouldn't that be a win-win scenario? It could work out positively for everyone. "You might be on to something, Rhona. But what would we stock? Who would we stock?"

Rhona clapped her hands and turned to the computer at the front desk. "Give me the rest of the day and I'll compile some designers and ideas for you. Then, if you give me the green light, I'll approach them and we'll get bespoke pieces in here pronto. They'd be mad to turn down showing here! You really have something truly unique, Lo."

"*We* have something unique, Rhonz."

Rhona smirked and puffed up her chest. She turned to the computer; her eyes focused on the task, a light illuminating within her.

After some hours had passed with two outfits sold to two American friends buying the same in different colours, Lori placed a cup of coffee on the desk, nudging Rhona out of her concentration.

"Wakey wakey!" She cooed. "You need a break, I can't be accused of imposing hard labour on my employee." Lori stretched her arms high above her after stitching up a bespoke skirt for a local, which she had gladly made the finishing touches to and placed on a hanger in the back cupboard ready for collection.

"There's a lot out there, Lori," Rhona took off her round-rimmed reading glasses. "So much incredible work... I'm actually in awe. Jeez, I wish I had an ounce of creativity." She let out a dramatic sigh, tearing her eyes away from the computer and rising from her seat. Joining Lori in stretching, she quickly grew bored and instead opted to lean on the table, sipping her cup of coffee.

"You are." Lori stretched her neck from side to side. "You organise this place; the flowers you bring in to make it beautiful, the window displays too! Whisht yourself!" Lori laughed and her friend immediately took the flattery with a confident flick of her short, dark hair.

Rhona launched into describing the top designers she had found. "It's whether you want to have a certain style in the shop... you could get pieces from across the globe to fit in with your aesthetic." Rhona pointed her pen to her scribbled notes. "There's a vegan leather maker in the south of France. Her bags would look divine thrown over one of your coats, plus the ethically handmade thing would fit in with your ethos. I can just see them selling like hot cakes." She took a breath, like a child too excited to keep calm. "It just depends what you would like." Rhona's sharp eyes examined her friend, but before Lori could even get a word in, she announced. "However, if *I* had to choose... I'd use designers within the Highlands. There are so many artisans sprawled over this place that I'm sure you'll find more than enough. And if all else fails, you can look further afield."

"Agreed!" Lori raised her hands. "You're on it, Rhonz, whatever you think. I trust you."

"I'm indeed on it. I'm your gal, darling!" Rhona bounced on the spot. "OK, there's a jewellery maker on the Isle of

Skye who has a stunning collection with exquisite gemstones, brooches, and necklaces." She placed her pen and notepad by the front desk. "I need to move...properly! Let's get some tunes on!" Rhona announced, marching to the sound system, where after several minutes of fiddling and swearing at her phone, a huge eruption of bagpipes, techno beats and everything in between hit Lori's ears.

"What is that?" Lori shouted over the strange jumble of musical instruments.

"Whoops!" Rhona tapped her phone, squinting at the device, then turned the volume even louder. "Feeling energised now?"

"Feeling I could hit a nightclub!" Lori laughed.

Rhona bobbed her head and pointed in the air with a silly expression on her face. She reached out and grabbed Lori's hand, pulling her into the small space next to the sewing machine, and continued bouncing on the spot.

"What's up with *your* face?" Rhona bellowed over the music.

Lori hesitated, remaining still. "Someone might walk in!"

"Oh, Jesus, Mary and Joseph!" Rhona threw up her hands, marched to the door, clicked the lock and marched back with an expectant look. "Well, my prim and proper employer, are you ready to let your hair down now?"

Lori giggled and moved her body, uncertain whether to do a Highland fling or shake her head in a frenzy. Rhona ignored her friend's hesitation and gyrated on the spot, giving all her energy into something replicating a Beyoncé routine. Lori let go of thoughts and wiggled her bum and moved the palm of her hands like a flapper girl. The energy of the music was infectious and soon she hopped onto her feet, as if she were at a ceilidh dance launching into some reel or other by herself. Rhona gave an outrageous cackle as she edged her bottom to the floor and pushed it out behind her like a pole dancer.

Then, to Lori's humiliation, a clean-shaven man stood by the front desk, watching the whole spectacle with a bemused smile. Lori stopped immediately, mortified. How had they not heard the doorbell? Caught off guard, her mouth open, she nudged Rhona, who was now trying her best at twerking but couldn't quite get the rhythm. She looked up; her bulging eyes taking in their unexpected visitor.

"I hope I'm not interrupting," he called, over sharp echoing bagpipes that were now in full swing with the beats.

Rhona fiddled with her phone, swearing in between, swiping until finally, silence fell, except for the mental shouting Lori unloaded on her friend: "Locked the door? My arse, you locked the door!" Fortunately, Rhona couldn't hear her inner rampage.

"Hi," said the stranger.

"Hi," Lori and Rhona said in unison.

"You're expecting me?" He placed his worn leather back-pack on the floor and Lori noticed a camera peeping from behind his back, its strap now noticeable across his chest. He shone with health, his face glowing with a sun-kissed complexion as he stood calmly, wearing an expectant expression on his face.

"*Are* we expecting you?" Lori blinked.

"I'm happy to expect *you*!" Rhona exclaimed, giving Lori a knowing look that caused her friend to blush.

"Did the magazine not say?" He ruffled his sandy hair, unaware of Rhona's inappropriate comment, and pulled out his phone, frowning at the screen.

Lori and Rhona looked at one another. "Magazine?"

"Yeah, for your featured interview," he responded, raising his camera with a smirk. "I'm here to capture photos of the new collection... and perhaps some shots of you." He extended his hand towards Rhona with a touch of old-fashioned charm. "But I can come back later and let you both continue dancing. Nice twerking, by the way!"

Lori was sure he was being cheeky.

Rhona bowed her head gracefully, agreeing with the statement. "There's room for one more."

"OK, let's go over this again," Lori cut through the flirting. "You're from a magazine?"

"I sure am. Not just any magazine – the number one fashion magazine in the world." He reached into his back pocket and produced his business card. Lori gawped at it. How was it possible that a photographer for the most prestigious fashion magazine ever to be published was knocking on her door?

He cast his eyes around the shop, allowing Lori time to adjust to the news. His focus slowed at Lori's mother's photo on the wall, then he turned his full attention back to Lori with a broad smile. "I'm Jack."

13

A fter a frantic phone call with the magazine's editorial assistant, Lori managed to piece together what had unfolded. They had sent her an email detailing a potential interview, assuming she had agreed to it. Searching through her junk folder, Lori stumbled upon the overlooked email, realising that the misunderstanding had originated from the assistant's end. She was well aware of the high-pressure environment that permeated the fashion industry, with its relentless workload and unforgiving deadlines. Nevertheless, the opportunity for her brand to gain worldwide exposure was too significant to pass up. Embracing the wave of Scottish appreciation that was sweeping through various forms of media, the magazine aimed to capture dramatic, ethereal photographs, with Lori's creations taking centre stage.

It was only when Lori put the phone down, she was hit with the realisation: what collection? She had nothing to show!

Jack left them to iron out the details and rambled around Morvaig, to get to know the "vibe" of the place.

"He's a right sexy wee bastard, that one." Rhona leaned over, startling Lori.

"Bloody hell, Rhona!" She gasped and spun round.

Rhona pouted at her reflection from her compact mirror. She applied red lipstick the moment Jack had left the shop. "He seems exotic, especially with that la-dee-dah posh accent!"

"Sh! Don't be saying things like that!" Lori whispered.

Rhona scoffed. "Oh please, he doesn't care. He seems more captivated by our 'charming town' than by little old me checking out his cute arse. I'm sure tongues will be wagging, especially at Katie's salon. People will be craning their necks at the window just to catch a glimpse of him."

Lori shook her head. "He's not that good-looking."

"He is. That skin, that hair, those arms. It's like he's stepped out of a costume drama with the way he speaks. Hello, Mr Darcy." She raised an eyebrow.

Lori scoffed. "He's just one of those photographers who never needed to try hard. I bet Daddy's money helped him get anywhere he wanted to go. I wouldn't be surprised if he shags all the models he photographs. It's despicable." Alarmed at what came out of her mouth, Lori consciously suppressed the rise of anger bubbling within her. She knew how the world could be easy for some – she'd experienced it first hand in New York.

"Oh, hello!" Rhona laughed. "Aren't we a little testy? Who cares what his story is, as long as he's polite, with a good heart... and a fine arse? Who are we to judge?"

Lori let out a groan in response. "Rhonz, we need to be professional. This is a huge deal, many designers spend their careers trying to get into this magazine... This has fallen into our laps!"

"I'm not the one judging the photographer!" Her eyes widened.

Lori's hands covered her face as she felt a surge of dread replace the photographer's distraction. How could she possibly produce a collection while Jack was there, given the limited timeframe? It would be physically impossible. "OK, I need help now, and I mean now – this very minute – there is just no way I can do this." She looked up at her friend in despair.

"OK." Rhona sobered up, her eyes darting from Lori to the phone, to the computer and back to Lori. Disappointingly, with no further point to add, she shrugged.

The bell above the door tinkled and in stepped the goth girl who had admired the shop some weeks earlier. She pulled down her sleeves, twisting the fabric between her black painted fingernails.

"Hi, Leanne, come in," Rhona called, and approached the timid girl. "How's your mum? It's her birthday soon. Are you in for a present?" She shimmied her into the shop.

Leanne nodded. "I saw some scarves in the window..." She chewed the inside of her mouth, standing awkwardly.

Rhona assisted the young girl and Lori stared at them both, her mind racing, and abruptly stood up from the front desk. "Leanne, is it? You were here before?"

The girl smiled.

Lori took in her appearance; it being the weekend, rather than her school uniform, she wore a cropped black jacket with a pleated detail at the back over a pair of high-waisted jeans. There was something unusual about her style – not gothic entirely, but an otherworldly appearance that was difficult to put into words.

"Did you make that coat yourself?" Lori smiled.

She shrugged. "Kind of. It was longer, and I altered it. It was my mum's."

"You can sew!" Rhona clapped her hands together.

"Only a little, I had to teach myself. I'm making a gown for my art class. I'm studying fashion history and the gown will go towards my final grade." She chewed the inside of her mouth again, her shoulders slightly hunched.

"Would you like to know how to sew better?" Lori knew this was her only option. She had little time for anything else and hoped against hope that this insecure teenager would be her saving grace.

"You're going to have to distract Jack for a bit." Lori pulled Rhona to the side as Leanne diligently followed Lori's instructions. She stitched simple seams of cheap fabric together until Lori could see how much training was required.

Rhona shook her head and pointed to her watch. "I can't, darling. I've got a ferry to catch." She shook her head with a chuckle. "Remember, I have kids waiting for me!"

"Oh yeah, that," Lori responded, her gaze fixed on the encroaching dusk outside the window.

"Just explain. I'm sure he'll be grand just exploring the area for a little while." Rhona clutched her handbag and zipped up her red waterproof anorak. "And you know I can't be here for the next few days – my kids need to see me!" She opened the door, letting in a gust of wind. She laughed heartily at Lori's daunted expression. "Darling, you've got this! I'll see you in a few days." A distant ferry horn boomed over the bay. "That's my ride, they're calling me!" Rhona waved and swiftly darted down the street, her red hood up, skilfully dodging puddles in her high heels.

Lori turned to Leanne who slowly unpicked some stitches she had made on a practise piece of cloth. This was going to be very difficult to pull off – training someone *and* make a collection, Lori thought miserably. She ventured into the back kitchen to get her thoughts in check. She rummaged in the fridge for a snack. Finding a pack of chocolate fingers, she opened the box and bit into the hard chocolate layer. Gazing out the small window by the microwave, she glimpsed a small red dot edging down the slip of the pier and safely onto the ferry. She clicked on the kettle and made a large plunger of coffee, filling it up to the brim. This was going to be a long night, but luckily for Lori, Leanne had called her mum to explain the situation, and with the guarantee of payment, she had agreed to the arrangement. Lori poured two large cups with a splash of milk and watched the ferry leave for the inner islands. No doubt Rhona would be happy to get away from the chaos of the shop... only to arrive at the chaos of her house!

I have got this. Lori straightened her back and plastered a smile on her face.

"I thought you had a collection ready? I was going to get the crew together, but now what am I to do?" Jack's expression was one of confusion rather than alarm, much to Lori's relief. But she had to confess her white lie. Eventually, he may have found out.

"I'm getting everything ready. We just need a little time."

"This is to go in our autumn edition, which means we need it approved pretty much ASAP." He leaned over Lori to see Leanne's head by the sewing machine. "Oh hello? You have help?" He looked back at Lori, a frown line appearing. "Look, it's not the end of the world. Just tell them, they could schedule you in for another time, maybe the next autumn or winter edition?"

"What? Are you serious? I can't waste this chance. Please! Can you not stretch out the time you need?" Lori pleaded, fully aware of how swiftly things could change in the world of magazines. Editors had the power to alter the course of publications, and various factors like job promotions, staff redundancies, and even the fleeting global appeal of Scotland could vanish before they even surfaced. She couldn't let this opportunity slip through her fingers. "There's a beautiful set of islands nearby. You could visit them, perhaps get some photographs, build up a story, or, better yet, visit the tweed mill where I get all my fabric from?" She tried to hide her desperate tone, but this was her chance to prove she could make her business a success. It was Callum's aunt who ran the tweed mill, and Lori was sure the eccentric woman would help her out in her hour of need.

Callum.

She needed to call him, but she didn't have time to dwell on him, not right now when her fashion label's future was at stake! Instead, she shrugged off the nagging uneasiness.

Jack took out his camera and fiddled with the lens. He moved his head side to side, weighing up the options. "Look, I don't want to take the piss with the magazine. They've been great at giving me work, and it's not fair to lie to them and keep them hanging on. It's risky. What if your collection doesn't look right in the setting? Sorry, but I'm just being honest." He casually took a photo of Leanne examining the sewing machine. "But what has really stumped me is that surely they already agreed which outfits would feature?"

He had a point.

"I believe they saw my statement pieces, like that one over there." Lori pointed to the flamboyant black number that had captured Leanne's imagination. "But I'll be showcasing so much more, that gown will look the least interesting piece in the entire collection!" Lori's instant confidence bowled even her over.

"Yeah, maybe, but I'm putting my neck out here. For what?"

Lori stopped. Of course, it was a risk; he was right. This wasn't just about her career. "I dunno." She shrugged, her confidence wavering.

He scratched his chin, then smoothed his fingers along his jawline. "Here's a thought: how about I interview you too? We chat about that photo over there." He pointed to her mother's photo on the wall.

She squinted at him. "You're a photographer, not a journalist."

He bobbed his head from side to side. "Yeah, but I may branch out. Also, if there's an extra story, it might help the feature."

"OK." Lori shrugged. "If that's what you want?"

"And dinner," his captivating gaze fixed on her.

"I'm not really sure that's a good idea." She hesitated, turning around in hopes of a distraction from Leanne at any moment; did she need help to cut fabric or sew a button? *No, nothing!* Her assistant remained quiet, making Lori feel stuck. Cornered. She couldn't help but feel flustered under Jack's unwavering attention. The way he looked at her with such directness had a disarming effect, leaving her slightly unsettled. What would she tell Callum? She tucked a stray hair behind her ear and Jack's dark eyes continued to study her, smiling at her reaction.

"It's just dinner. We need to get to know each other better. It might be good to get your thoughts on the photo shoot too." He adjusted his camera strap over his shoulder.

Lori couldn't really refuse him after already asking such a favour from him. And he was right. They needed to form their working relationship. It made sense. Purely professional. If Callum could fix a past girlfriend's washing machine and spend nights celebrating in the pub together, then she could have dinner with a colleague. It may just give her an insight into the magazine business, helping to propel her career. Never mind that Jack was gorgeous, to other women, at least. What's the worst that could happen?

"Why not? OK, let's have dinner." Lori agreed and turned to her helper who remained quiet. Leanne's head snapped down as she fumbled with the stitch ripper.

If Lori didn't know better, she would have thought her young friend had been listening to their conversation all along.

14

L ori sat at the kitchen table, immersed in her latest designs. She lifted her gaze from the sketches and watched her gran shuffling around the kitchen in her pink flamingo-covered kimono. Gran poured herself a cup of tea and gazed out at the rain-soaked back garden with a contented sigh. The blustery wind whipped debris against the window, leaving raindrops trailing down the glass.

"Someone's in a good mood!" Lori grinned, feeling positively giddy herself; her designs were coming together nicely, and with Leanne's sewing help, she was looking forward to the photo shoot.

"Aren't I always in a good mood?" Gran tittered and sat next to Lori at the kitchen table. "You missed a good meeting last night."

Ever since discovering the last-minute news about her impending photo shoot, Lori had been forced to scale back on all other distractions in her life. This included, to her great relief, committee meetings.

"Really? Do tell, Gran."

"Mr Green dropped by again. He thought he had the better of me; apparently I stipulated there would be no further meeting to take a vote on council plans for an allotment next to the high school. We found the minutes of the meeting he was talking about and I said nothing of the sort!" She scoffed, crossing her legs.

"Sounds riveting."

"Excuse me, Mrs. 'I have no time for anything other than haute couture!'" Gran squinted at Lori's sketches. "Although, I must admit, they do look... rather beautiful." Her index finger tapped the design inspired by the fisherman's outfit. "When all this hectic business is over, perhaps you could make this in my size?"

"Of course, Gran," Lori giggled. "But where would you wear it? It's fancy for round here."

"Who's to say I won't travel again?" She raised an eyebrow. "I can walk now, more often without those ridiculous sticks. A little plane journey wouldn't be so bad." She smoothed her hand down her neck, sitting upright. "We may even have some glamorous events coming up here. Who knows? I think if you want something, it's always a good idea to get it." Gran patted Lori's cheek. "Make any excuse to wear them!" She smiled. "Now, if you'll excuse me, I have another meeting to attend to."

"Another one? But that's three times in the last week!" Lori called after her gran, but the old woman dismissed her with a playful wave.

Lori sat open-mouthed. Bracken appeared and placed his heavy head on her lap. She patted his fur absentmindedly. She had watched something new in Gran, but what was it? Now thinking about her gran's words, her walking *had* improved, as well as her overall mood. She seemed different somehow. A little more energetic than Lori had seen in many months, which left her even more perplexed as to the reason for her change. Her gran kept to her routines and hadn't done anything more than attend those dull committee meetings, arguing with the odious Mr Green...

Maybe she was putting too much thought into it. Her gran was gaining more confidence with her energy and fitness levels.

That was it. That had to be it.

Callum was in high spirits since scoring the last point for their team. He smashed the ball at such speed, the goalie hadn't even realised what had happened until it was too late and the referee blew the whistle. The game was over, and they emerged victorious by a single point. Overwhelmed by a mix of astonishment and elation, Callum accepted the pats on the back from his teammates. Then, almost oblivious to his surroundings, his two teammates lifted him up, hoisted him in the air, and danced around like gleeful eejits. They had their third win since starting their Highlands tour, and if they kept this up, with any luck, they would win the tournament. Even Callum's least favourite teammate, Ryan, had shaken his hand weakly and mumbled congratulations. The gesture, as awkward as it was, made Callum feel even more smug.

"Pub!" Alan shouted in the changing rooms to cheers from their teammates. "If it wasn't for Cal here, we'd be sore losers now." He thumped his friend affectionately on the back, his strength always surprising Callum, and this time it left a dull pain tingling up his back.

"Jeez, Alan, I'm too old for this," Callum said quietly. "We've celebrated the last few nights. Let's just have a quiet one: a rich stodgy meal and bed. I've been thinking about steak pie all day."

Alan shook his head and scoffed. "Oh, come on, you oldie. Tomorrow's game might be a different story – this could be our last hoolie!"

Callum sighed to himself. If they had an early night, their chances of winning would be far greater than staggering onto the pitch hungover. His partying days were slowly coming to a halt, unlike his friend, who had an abundance of energy... and a wife and baby at home. If it was Callum's choice, he'd find it difficult to leave home as often as Alan. But whatever worked for a couple – it wasn't for him to judge. He threw his damp towel down and pulled on jeans, catching his reflection in an open locker mirror. His body had been through such vigorous exercise, and if he wasn't careful, he would regret not looking after himself. He was fit. There was no problem with that, but he ached in places he'd never known existed. Being the eldest in the team, he knew he needed to slow down soon and not give in to peer pressure. He had seen Lori doing yoga some evenings before bed, but there was only so much watching her bending and stretching he could endure before he had to take her to bed with him. But perhaps if he tried something similar, it might help him keep up with the younger lads.

Only a few more days of focusing on the game, then he could start his business plan. The hours spent on the bus driving from one match to the next had put things into perspective for Callum. He'd had a brainwave; it had been lurking for some time, but finally came to the forefront when he discussed some ideas with the local MP. After their last match, the MP approached him with congratulations, and Callum, being so taken aback at their unlikely supporter, had somehow got into a discussion on employment in the Highlands. He'd mentioned his own business idea and, to his surprise, it had come across well researched and thought out. It may just work. If he focused on getting through the rest of their shinty tour, he could start planning in earnest on his return home.

He reached into his pocket and pulled out his phone. If he was to go to the pub with the boys, now was the time to check in with Lori. No answer. Likely she was out walking, perhaps with little Rory.

Callum imagined Lori marching up and down hills with the little lad strapped to her, blissfully content. He was a funny wee thing, and Lori was good with him, if a little uncertain. But she doted on him in her own way.

Callum tucked the phone away and pulled on his hoodie with the team's symbol: a white stag. Even after the hot shower, he was still cold. He needed to act fast if he was to train his body to withstand the brutal punishment of being kicked and hit on the field. It was time for a change. He'd work things out soon – start afresh and also make more time for Lori. Their departure had been strange and a little chaste. Their carefree travels together seemed such a long time ago. But things would work out, Callum was sure of it – they would work through whatever problems came their way, surely?

Whatever seemed to be going on in her head of late left him puzzled. It was like she was so distracted by her business, plunging headlong into things, that she had little brain power left for him. But it would blow over. She was making the business profitable and soon would be back to normal. What irked him, if he really thought about it, was that she took every minor obstacle that came her way personally. He hoped in time she would trust in her own abilities.

He left the steam-filled changing room, throwing his sports bag over his shoulder. Instead of boarding the bus with his teammates, he opted to walk the short distance to the hotel. As he waved off their playful obscenities from the bus, he relished the opportunity to spend some time alone. Being on his own had always been his comfort zone - a chance to be with his own thoughts and enjoy the freedom to do as he pleased. However, lately, he had realised that more people had entered his life, and it wasn't something he complained about. His parents and sister were busy with their own lives, but the Robertsons had warmly embraced him as part of their family. Despite this, now that he was there, things didn't quite unfold as he had anticipated. Although surrounded by people, he couldn't shake the feeling that something was missing. Pushing those thoughts aside, he resolved to revisit them later and instead focused on his new business plan—a potential solution to all their problems.

He reached the hotel just as the bus was slowly coming to a stop.

"Lazy lumps ye all are!" He snorted at his teammates, who sheepishly stepped off the bus.

"You can't blame us. We've been on our feet all day!" One of the newer players announced with a grin.

"Here's me thinking I'm the old one!" Callum shook his head.

"You are the old one!" Alan glided past him and gave a playful push, making Callum's back twitch in the same spot as before. "But you're the best shot this side of Scotland, so we'll keep you, old and haggard as you are!" He winked and continued into the warm glow of the pub.

Callum rubbed his back discreetly.

15

"I wish you would come..." Lori pleaded over the phone and ran another handful of mousse through her curls in an attempt to tame them.

"Oh yeah, I'm sure he would be absolutely *thrilled* if I showed up!" Rhona scoffed into the phone, then immediately switched gears and barked, "Charlene, if you don't give your brother back his precious GI Joe, I swear I'll take away your beloved Barbie piece by piece. I mean it! Her shoes will vanish, her dresses will disappear, and even that sparkly red tiara will be gone! And I'll do it when you least expect it!" She yelled at her eldest child, who had dared to answer her back. "That's it, I warned you. Charlene! No, don't do that—it's his favourite toy! Alright, on the count of three, you better release GI Joe!"

Lori winced on the other end, the tension palpable as she imagined little Charlene holding the plastic toy perilously close to an open flame. A few moments of silence passed before Lori whispered, "Everything okay?"

"Okay, good girl, that's right," Rhona encouraged, her voice laced with relief. "Now, just give it back to your brother... Charlene!" She barked, frustration seeping into her tone. "Tell me, Lori, why did I ever think having a girl was a good idea? She's ageing me, I tell you. Ageing me! I swear, last night I discovered three new wrinkles around my eyes. Three! On each side... that's a grand total of six! And don't even get me started on my forehead!" Rhona groaned, exasperation evident in her voice.

"Please come tonight, Rhona. Sounds like you need a break!" Lori begged.

"I can't! And as I said, Jack doesn't want to see me."

"What do you mean? You're part of the business. It's a business-dinner meeting," Lori panicked midway through applying mascara, and jabbed her eye with the stick. "Ouch!"

"Lo, I hope you're not applying makeup over the phone. You'll end up with only half your face made up! I should know, been there and done it! Now breathe... you're getting all excited."

"I... I just want to be professional. It's a big deal, this magazine. I want to make a good impression on Jack."

"You'll be fine, you're a total boss babe. There's no harm in a little flirt. It keeps things exciting."

"I'm not flirting. I've actually been the opposite. Honestly, Rhona, please come, you'd get a fancy meal - I'll buy you the most expensive thing on the menu... lobster!"

"Oh, Lo, I have lobsters coming out of my ears. I get a batch every other week from Gerry the ferryman, who gets them from his brother—"

"Okay, okay!" Lori quickly interjected, not wanting to be subjected to a barrage of names she had no interest in hearing. "What I meant was, you deserve to have a lovely evening. Please come!"

"Sorry, there's only one ferry over, and I can't leave the

kids tonight. My middle one has been having night terrors and wetting the bed. Anyhoo, I don't want to be a third wheel in whatever flirtations are going on."

"Don't say that! There's nothing more than—"

"I know, I know, a professional acquaintance? Well, according to your wee intern, there were sparks flying!"

Lori had treasured the sheer determination behind Leanne's quiet demeanour, but the young girl appeared to have some undesirable qualities, such as being another member of the local gossip brigade! "I can see I'll need to keep an eye on Leanne. She should not be telling silly stories and spreading them around the area. I have a boyfriend, for Christ's sake!"

"Na, Leanne wouldn't. I may have badgered it out of her. Don't be hard on the girl, she's a good sausage!"

Lori's tightened shoulders relaxed a little. Knowing her friend was a little on the pushy side, especially to extract any details, it seemed a far more convincing story. Although she hadn't the slightest idea how a girl being a sausage had anything to do with it.

Lori made her way to the restaurant a little early to get a drink to calm her nerves. Since Jack had showed up in her shop, needing an urgent fashion collection, it had left Lori somewhat jittery. She sat at the shiny wooden bar, sipping vodka and lime, and texted Callum.

> *"Hey, sorry I missed your call. Things are good*
> *here! Luckily, Leanne is sewing up a storm*
> *for the collection. Busy but good. Well done on*

winning the game, we'll need to celebrate
when you're back. L x"

Lori switched off her phone and drummed her fingers on the bar counter. With her back to the restaurant, she could feel the movement of servers darting back and forth to the kitchen, amidst the continuous chatter of customers with sporadic bouts of laughter. Lori allowed her mind to wander as she observed the few patrons at the bar, consisting mostly of elderly men engrossed in their newspapers or fixated on the television screen above. In the far corner, a captivating painting of a majestic ship crashing into waves caught her eye. However, it was the figure seated beneath it, nursing a glass of dark liquor, that held her gaze: Mr. Green, the angry busybody who disrupted the community council's meetings. Yet, on this particular evening, he appeared distinct from his usual stern self - his features sagging and lifeless. He sipped his drink, lost in thought and gazing into the distance, isolated from the chatter of other patrons his age. Despite their friendly banter, he remained aloof. There was something about his posture and the faraway look in his eyes that seemed so pitiful, Lori couldn't help but feel the tiniest bit sorry for him. If he wasn't so odious to her gran, she might have suggested he joined her for a drink, but judging by his body language, and the other local men's disregard for him in the corner, he may have been rude to more people than just her gran.

He gazed into his drink, his eyes reddening, then, without warning, those piercing eyes snapped up to meet hers. Caught! Why was she staring at him? Now things would be even more awkward between them, like they weren't awkward before! She remembered his accusation at her being part of the committee because of her gran's ulterior motives.

Lori breathed out, psyching herself for a meeting she was reluctant to have, but she needed to say something to him, be the better woman...

"Well, hello there." Jack sat next to Lori, placing his camera bag over the chair and got the barman's attention. "I'll have a lager, and the same again for the lady?"

Lori nodded in thanks, momentarily distracted by the new arrival.

"So I'm not the only one who likes to arrive early."

Lori chuckled. "Apparently not. Although you do like to come unannounced too!"

"Ah yes, well we got that misunderstanding all ironed out. I would have thought you'd be happy that I showed up!" He raised his hands. "Anyway, I just go where I'm sent. I let others do the planning. But things look like they're coming together for the photo shoot?" He took a sip from his glass, his eyes lingering on Lori.

She smiled but looked back at the corner painting. Instead of Mr Green's gloomy countenance, only an empty glass remained.

Jack followed her gaze. "Everything OK?"

Lori shifted in her seat. "Yes, fine... I just thought I saw someone," she lied.

Jack watched her for a moment before casting his eyes back to the corner. "Nice painting. Atmospheric, reminds me of Turner... with a hint of Rupert Bunny thrown in," he remarked and took another sip from his glass.

Lori was impressed. "You know Rupert Bunny's work?" she asked. After her time in Australia and New York, Lori's social calendar had been filled with fashion events and soirées, mostly related to her work or her ex-fiancé Michael.

However, there were occasional moments when they would attend art gallery openings together, allowing Lori to indulge in her love for art. Meeting the artists and experiencing new exclusive works or classic historical pieces up close thrilled her. Art became her escape, particularly during a time when she felt a lack of real creativity in her own work.

"Yeah, I've been around." He chuckled. "I saw an exhibition in Melbourne. I find his work really inspiring; it's bizarre that he's not very well known. People just don't have taste, I guess." He shrugged.

Lori reflected on the paintings she had seen at the same show in Melbourne. The dreamy quality of mermaids and other mythology subjects stayed with her even now. It tapped into something deep within her, so much so that she carried a small cut-out print of a painting. She opened her purse and went into the small flap that she had never used. Unfolding the crumbled image; a man and woman leaning against one another, staring off across the water, the man playing a flute, surrounded by frolicking half-naked fairies, mermaid or nymphs.

Jack laughed. "No way. You went to the same show! That must have been... years ago!"

"About ten years, I'd say." Lori smiled and carefully tucked the cut-out back into her purse.

"What are the chances of that happening? I mean, maybe we were even there on the same day, standing side by side looking at the same piece!" He thumped the bar counter in disbelief, his eyes bright.

Lori shrugged, but noted it was strange. Although these things happened all the time. What really hit her, was just how long she hadn't talked about art. It was something she never spoke of with Callum. Not that she missed it, it was just different.

Lori experienced a strange sensation, as if a wave washed over her. For a moment, she felt pulled in two directions - a desire to leave and a desire to stay. She wasn't entirely certain about what she should do.

Jack held her gaze for a few moments. "Actually, I'm certain I would have noticed you."

Mid-sip, Lori choked on her drink, almost swallowing an ice cube in surprise. She spluttered, and Jack handed her a tissue. She blushed while trying to compose herself. Then a loud noise erupted behind them; a dinner party laughing at a joke. Lori was glad of the disturbance and shook herself. What was the matter with her? She was a grown woman and didn't need to act like a silly airhead who couldn't take a compliment. *An innocent compliment, that was all.*

As much as she emphasised their acquaintance was purely for business, she thought it wise to have only one more drink at dinner and leave as early as possible.

A red-faced server announced their table was ready, and Jack stood up, allowing Lori to go ahead and briefly touched her elbow. Nothing more than a light graze, but the gesture had caught her off guard. There was a protective admiration in his body language that made Lori stand a little taller.

16

As Lori approached the shop the next morning, a relentless headache pounded in her temples - a headache that, surprisingly, hadn't been alleviated by one of Gran's famed bacon sandwiches. And there, amidst the chaos of her throbbing head, stood Rhona, already hard at work. With a duster in one hand and a spray bottle in the other, she was a whirlwind of activity, dressed in a deep red headscarf and bold red lipstick.

"How was dinner?" Rhona casually tossed the duster over her shoulder, not bothering to look as it gracefully landed in the wash basin behind her. Leaning provocatively over the table, she exuded an air of intrigue, eagerly awaiting Lori's response.

Lori took a shaky sip from her bottle of water and surveyed her friend from afar, not truly convinced Rhona had been cleaning at all, but awaiting her arrival for details. "It was nice," she croaked, her voice strained, as she slowly took a seat at the front desk.

Rhona leaned in closer, her curiosity evident. "Uh-huh, and?" She prodded, eager for more details.

Lori tapped on her phone and realised there were no messages from Callum. A tinge of disappointment washed over her.

"What? Is that all I'm getting?" Rhona's mouth gaped open in outrage. "I took the early ferry over too, you know. And all I get is 'it was nice'? Seriously! I should have stayed home and watched that morning TV show. They had an eighty-year-old man who married his dog and a mother of two who can't stop eating furniture."

"What?"

"Yeah, I know! Now I'll never get to see them, and that kind of telly doesn't come around too often, Lo!" She folded her arms and slumped against the cutting table.

Lori tapped the keyboard, waiting for the computer to start up. She grunted again. "I drank too much."

"I can see that!"

Lori spun around in the swivel chair. "Rhona, what does a girl have to do to get a drink round here?"

"Don't you think you've had enough, darling? Although, on second thoughts maybe the old 'hair of the dog' is a good idea. My mother-in-law swears by it. You know every Christmas morning she makes me a—"

"Coffee, Rhona, I meant coffee," Lori said wearily, resting her head on her arm.

"Oh yes, sure!" Rhona chuckled. "I'll head down the road and get us a cuppa. Need to show off these pins anyway!" She stretched out her legs to show a sexy black line up the back of her calves.

"Wait!" Lori ordered, hastily draping a red tweed cape across Rhona's shoulders. The addition highlighted her look immensely as she sauntered out the front door, exuding the aura of a movie star.

"Please don't say it was *nice* again," Rhona groaned on her return, handing Lori a paper cup.

"It was."

"I'm taking that coffee away this instant!" she threatened, her hand outstretched.

"No, wait." Lori clutched her life raft. "OK, it was great. We decided on where the photo shoot would be, which models to use, makeup and hair, and the overall theme of the shoot. It really was a very productive meeting."

"I can see that. And did you drink the whole restaurant dry?"

"No, we just had some wine with dinner," Lori replied, her voice tinged with hesitation. It wasn't precisely a lie, yet it wasn't entirely the truth either, as Lori reluctantly acknowledged. They had stayed in the restaurant until closing, then moved to the pub next door for a nightcap. Their discussion of the photoshoot had been so much fun that Lori could hardly wait for the day to come. They appeared to agree on what they wanted to capture, and Lori had to admit she'd been entirely wrong about Jack. There was so much more to him than he let on, and he fascinated her professionally. "He's very talented. He showed me his work. He's an artist, you know, he paints as well as being a photographer and he works freelance. Isn't that pretty awesome?"

Rhona raised her eyebrows.

"Jack doesn't work solely for anyone. He lives in London, where he has a studio, and then takes trips across the world. He said he's always wanted to come up here, so when the magazine approached him, he jumped at it. Isn't that pretty great? He gets to do the jobs he really wants to do." Lori smiled to herself.

"And he really wanted to do this one?"

Lori's mind drifted back to the conversation she had shared with Jack during their dinner the previous evening. The realisation that he had been aware of her even before the magazine had approached him, left her astounded.

"It was crazy. I read an article that said you guys had won an award. I googled your work and loved the imagery of the shop and felt drawn to it. Then the next day I get a call asking if I'd be interested in taking some shots of your work. It's strange, but if I'm honest... I took it as a sign. It all felt very serendipitous. I just couldn't refuse."

Having relaxed in Jack's company, Lori found herself captivated as he spoke about the freedom he enjoyed in his work. She soaked in the wondrous adventures he shared, realising how appealing his life sounded. Since leaving the city to live in the countryside, Lori had missed more than she had initially admitted.

Rhona's cough interrupted her thoughts, bringing Lori back to the conversation. "You both sounded like you *did* have a nice dinner..." Rhona commented, prompting Lori to nod and offer a faint smile in agreement.

"Yeah."

"OK, something's going on. You've got a weird look in your eye."

"Nothing went on. Rhona, I have a boyfriend! We just had a really great time discussing our interests and realising we have a lot in common." Lori also couldn't ignore the fact that she was drawn to Jack. But as amazing as it was to be with a kindred spirit, it might be wise to not spend anymore one-on-one time with him.

The shop bell rang, and Leanne ducked her head with her shy smile.

"You're early!" Rhona stood up and helped Leanne take off her black jacket.

"Thought I'd come in, I have a free period this morning. I really want to see how you embellish the swing skirt. I've been embroidering and trying beadwork for my portfolio, but it's really difficult... and so slow. I hoped I might see your secret?" She pulled at her long sleeves awkwardly.

Lori waved her finger at Leanne. "This is why I like this girl, she's always keen to learn." The more time Lori spent with the teenager, the more she realised that the timid girl was a fast learner. Despite her lack of confidence in her abilities, Leanne consistently exceeded Lori's expectations with each task she undertook. And since she had confided to Lori and Rhona that she was hoping to apply to art school, it became more apparent that her working there benefitted her just as much as Lori.

"If it's fashion-related, then yes please. I want to know everything!" Leanne marched to the back kitchen and shortly reappeared with a cup of tea in hand and a determined look in her eye. She took a sip, then began unpacking a box of fabric, placing various tubes of jewel-coloured beads on the cutting table, along with Lori's prized sewing box. Leanne spun round to Lori. "Ready!"

"OK, let's start!" Lori chuckled and sat down next to the young girl. She retrieved chalk from her sewing box and unfolded sections of white fabric. Leanne observed Lori's example of selecting beads and the technique she employed to apply them to the fabric.

Lori grinned at her apprentice, pondering how she had already become a teacher in her career. She was still in the process of learning herself, considering she had only been running the business for less than a year. It felt surreal to imagine she was making things work, after all. She dedicated her free time to researching new techniques to keep abreast with new fashions and perfecting her skills in dressmaking. High above her mother's sewing machine, a thick solid shelf was crammed with tailoring and dressmaking books, which had proved more than a good read. They were making her into a far better craftswoman than she had ever thought possible. The prospect of being featured in one of the largest fashion magazines in the world, alongside high-end fashion labels, made her dizzy.

Rhona squealed and clapped her hands when the delivery man unloaded several boxes labelled for the shop.

"Lori, you have to see this!" Rhona exclaimed, grabbing a pair of scissors and swiftly cutting open the first box. Gasping in excitement, she pulled out an array of bags and boxes, each containing luxurious treasures: belts, intricately woven leather bags, hats adorned with fluffy pompoms, and vibrant, shiny jewellery. Rhona bounced with anticipation, showcasing long feather earrings that cascaded down to her shoulders. Her enamoured audience murmured oohs and ahhs at the demonstration, clapping for more.

"Boho chic." Leanne nodded with approval. "And... it would go great with this." She pulled a fringed-edged cape off a hanger.

"I could model it for you? I can drape myself over a tree branch or frolic on the beach," Rhona suggested with a pout, peeking out from behind the garment that Leanne held up.

"You have great taste, Rhonz," Lori gazed into boxes, shaking her head in awe. "I can't believe these are fairly local!"

"Yup, who would've thought it? Now you are showcasing other designers' work... pretty amazing!" She nudged her friend playfully. "Now if you'll excuse me, I have to record all these items, pop them on our website, respond to emails, and get them priced up!"

"We'll not disturb you." Lori pulled Leanne away from a rainbow of bracelets.

"I think I'll still be here this time next week!" Rhona sighed, happily sorting the pieces while humming a tune, a smile illuminating her face.

"Well hello." Jack popped his head around the shop door. "I hope I'm not disturbing you?"

"No, not at all!" Lori marched up to meet him, leaving her student to stitch the final beads on a hemmed skirt. Leanne peeked from behind the mannequin, scanning their new arrival, but went back to pulling a needle of long thread, looping another bead and stitching it down.

"Wow, is this for the shoot?" He approached Leanne, whose serious face remained fixed on the garment.

"It is." Lori took him to the freshly pressed garments draped on hangers behind the cutting table. "These are the other pieces." Lori beamed like a proud mother.

"Wow," he uttered again. "You have been busy."

Lori showed him each piece. "I think these would really work, especially with our theme."

Jack snapped a photo of Lori sifting through the clothes, her hands resting on each piece gently, lovingly. Lori looked up at him, surprised.

"I couldn't resist. I hope you don't mind." He sheepishly lowered his lens. "You are quite a vision..."

Leanne peered around the mannequin again, this time wearing a frown.

"I mean... these clothes look... what I mean is the article

could use more behind-the-scenes shots. Particularly with our theme now confirmed, I think imagery with you... your red hair, will look outstanding."

They both laughed but stayed in close proximity to one another.

"What *is* your theme?" Rhona popped her head around the corner, her eyebrow raised.

Lori smoothed a hand through her curls and scratched the back of her neck. "It's going to be dreamy... inspired by the work of an Australian artist: Rupert Bunny," Lori said to Rhona's blank expression.

Jack watched her for a moment. "I can't wait."

17

Callum shook the estate agent's hand. The man dipped his tweed cap respectfully and hopped into his Land Rover, leaving Callum to process what had just happened. They had a gentleman's agreement – Callum would buy a large plot of land in the rural area surrounding Arlochy. The land in question hadn't been worth the time, or so the agent advised, and was more work than income. So the landlord divided it into sections and was selling it off. Callum had never come across such a deal where he could buy land, especially in his local area, so he almost snapped the agent's hand off there and then. There was a catch, however, as stipulated by the landlord, the agreement needed investment and 'to give something back' to the land. Callum suggested planting trees and the offer was taken. He laughed to himself, dizzy with adrenaline at the sheer expanse around him and the opportunities it offered. He pictured an idyllic life, in which he could create a natural habitat, replanting native trees that once belonged to the land, and as a result, bringing back animals and native species. Callum made a promise to himself and the landlord that none of the trees he planted would get cut down. Most of the forests that remained in the Highlands were temporary, their trunks marked and sold for timber. He had often gone to High Arlour, a woodland with hidden secrets that led walkers towards an old clearance village up in the hills. Those people, who had left their village centuries ago, were driven away by a multitude of reasons, leaving their homes to the elements, which over time had turned them into clumps of scattered rocks. Despite its sad history, High Arlour was one of his favourite spots to roam and seek the forest's solitude. And as Callum aged, so did those trees. They continued to thrive and heal the old wounds left by the ruins. Their protective branches created their own ecosystem, keeping the site sacred and shielding it from the changing world outside. But as he continued to age, the trees did not and were cut down, logged and sold. When he walked through that empty place now, a desert of trees ripped open, he felt a grief for all that was gone. They stunted life and drove it away on trucks, all for a quick buck. Well, he would not let it happen to this project. This land.

He saw the possibilities of building his own home and, perhaps, creating a sustainable business that offered eco-friendly accommodation where nature and humans could live in harmony as they once did. Ideas filled his head. Buzzing with excitement, he ran up a sheep track to the top of the hill overlooking even more hills. He turned to see a loch further down the glen. A loch once full of trout, which he and friends would fish for in their teenage years.

The area was remote, situated at the end of a tourist track that hugged the shoreline of the loch and ascended the hill toward an overgrown old church. Occasionally, a hiker could be seen studying a map, but there was little else to draw people to the area. Callum, captivated by the presence of ancient civilisations that had once inhabited such forgotten places, marvelled at how time had reclaimed them, with wild grass now engulfing their remnants, leaving only stone structures behind. He rubbed his hands together. There was a lot of work to do, but a blank slate to work from. This was what he'd been waiting for. His recent hesitations had haunted him, making him worry if he had made a wise decision about giving up his *Adventurous Tours* after all. Now he could see he needed to give up the business to make way for a new adventure. Clear the old and in with the new.

He had been at the same spot for a few hours, and each time he roamed the hill, a vivid image consumed his thoughts: Lori, approaching him with a baby cradled in her arms, a loving smile on her face, welcoming him home after a long day's work. They would be happy here. He was sure Lori, with her ambitious energy, would be delighted to watch this new venture take shape. He should have told her, but he couldn't risk the landlord selling it to another. The agent had already revealed that the landlord had considered offering the plot to the adjoining estate owner. Callum needed to act fast and plan later. Lori would understand, especially when she saw the location. They could make space for family members – Gran, Alan and Tammy, even Jean and the girls. Everyone could live on the land in their own lodges. It was a big dream, but he would make it happen. He would find a way.

Callum hiked the marshland and scouted the whole area they had agreed on. Seeing it in person, it felt far larger than he had seen on paper. It would take time, but this would be good for the whole family, and he couldn't wait to get started.

Callum drove towards Arlochy village, taking a deep breath in and out, calming his thoughts before sheer adrenaline took over. His phone rang loudly, breaking him out of his meditation. Glancing at the screen, he saw the name "Fran." He paused for a moment, contemplating whether to answer. His friend had been reaching out to him frequently lately, asking for favours, and he was always willing to lend a hand. However, with each call came another task, and considering his current situation, Callum had very little time to take on any more unpaid jobs for others. Since he helped Fran with her washing machine, he'd received a request from her elderly neighbour who needed help to carry a new fridge upstairs. Then even more people had heard of his handyman skills. As much as Callum wanted to help people out now and then, he didn't want to make it a career, not when he had a large plot of land needing his attention. He would just need to tell Fran. Surely, she would understand his situation, but a part of him still felt compelled to assist her. Despite the growing list of tasks, she had been there for him when he needed support the most. She had helped him overcome his emotional slump after Jennifer's departure, and for that, he would always be grateful.

Callum pulled over to the side of the road and parked his car. Taking a deep breath, he answered the call. "Fran, how are you?"

"Cal-cal! Thank god you're there! Are you still on your shinty trip? I don't suppose you're home?"

"I'm home, well, just about! I left the boys a little earlier than planned."

"Oh goodie, please please, please could you help me? Water has covered my kitchen floor. I think some pipe has sprung a leak!" She squeaked, then an abrupt noise resembling a strangled cat sounded.

"Everything OK?"

"Ah, blast it! Yeah, ouch! I slipped, I think my ankle is... Ouch!"

"I'm coming now!" Callum sped towards Fran's house as fast as he could. When he got there, he let himself in with his copy of keys and found Fran lying on the sofa watching tv.

"Are you OK?" he shouted over the loud game show music, as the contestants tried to decipher some riddle on a flashing board.

Fran sighed and pressed the remote control, lowering the volume of the audience's applause. She looked up at him sheepishly. "I think so, it just hurts a bit. But please, Cal-Cal, the kitchen floor... it's awful!"

He rushed into the kitchen, his footsteps splashing through the water on the floor. Spotting the water spraying from under the sink, he reacted instantly. Without wasting a moment, he dove under the sink, snatched a towel, and tightly wrapped it around the pipe, stopping the flow of water.

"Have you any tools? A spanner or something?" he shouted to Fran, who remained on the sofa.

"No, Cal, I'm not a handyman. No tools in this household."

Callum tutted to himself. It looked like there was more damage than just the pipe. *I'm not a handyman either!* He tied the towel around the spraying pipe and darted to his van, hoping he had something there that would help. He found a large rusty spanner, along with a bag of tools he thought he'd given away long ago. Callum went back into the kitchen and rolled up his shirt sleeves. This was going to take him away from Lori. He had wanted to surprise her a day earlier than expected. But with Fran hurt on the sofa, and her house flooded, he had no choice but to help his old friend.

18

Lori hugged Leanne tightly, and the two of them squealed with joy, swaying back and forth.

"I can't believe we did it. We actually did it, Leanne!"

"They look amazing, Lori. I can't wait to see this one on a model!" Leanne touched black netting, beneath which meters of silk fabric gathered in tight pleats, skimming the floor. The vibrant green and turquoise colours stood out against the backdrop of other hues, resembling a peacock's feathers. Lori had invested a substantial amount of money in fabric and was relieved to see her vision come to life. She wholeheartedly agreed with her apprentice; the outfit would look absolutely stunning on a model, wandering gracefully through the moorland.

"I just wish you could come tomorrow. There will be a whole team there! Makeup artist, hair stylist, models!"

"I know." Leanne sighed, her face downcast. Her mother had insisted that under no circumstance would Leanne miss school to help with the collection. Her studies must come first and school was the priority, which Lori could understand. Ahead of her years as she may seem, Leanne needed to focus on her education.

"Don't worry. I'll take a lot of behind-the-scenes footage." Lori nodded as she let her friend out the door before locking up. "Now have a good night, you!"

"I will." Leanne stepped into the early evening light. "Make sure you keep me updated. I want to know everything!" She sauntered off with a skip and kicked a loose stone across the street, smiling to herself.

Lori locked the front door and took another look at their collection. She had neatly placed everything on hangers, labelled and pressed to perfection. A surge of pride welled up within her. They had truly outdone themselves this time.

She let down her hair and massaged her scalp, closing her eyes. She hadn't dared to acknowledge the exhaustion that crept over her, but now that everything was safely prepared for the photo shoot, she could finally relax. Lori switched off the lights and packed away her belongings. A sharp thumb on the door made her jump.

"Let us in." Rhona pressed her face at the window and left a pink lipstick kiss on the glass.

"Hey, you'll need to wash that!" Lori crossed her arms, leaning against the open door. "What's all this?"

Rhona, Gran, and Tammy, with Rory in a sling, greeted her.

"You all look wonderful. Is there a black-tie event I wasn't invited to?" Lori snorted.

"I thought you might forget, since you've steered away from the committee meetings" – Gran eyed her under purple spectacles – "tonight is one of our charity fundraisers." Gran clasped her hands together with a sigh. "Not to worry. We'll meet you there, shall we?"

Lori panicked. "Oh, Gran, I thought I might get an early

night. It's the fashion shoot tomorrow and I need to have a clear head."

"Oh, no you don't," Tammy insisted. "I haven't been out in public since I was the size of a house. I don't want anyone thinking I put on weight. I want them to see there was a reason behind it all," Tammy whispered.

"Tam, everyone knew you were pregnant. It was obvious. Plus, small town means big gossip! Right, Rhona?" Lori nudged her friend, who nodded with a knowing smile.

"Come on, Lori, let's not leave these lovely ladies waiting." Rhona quickly ushered her flustered friend back into the shop.

"But I've nothing to wear, and what are we even attending?" Lori wrung her hands. "I just want an early night. Doesn't everyone know how hard I've been working?"

Rhona placed her hands on Lori's arms, led her to the swivel chair and pushed her down to sit. "OK, Lori, I think it's best I tell you. Are you listening?"

Lori nodded gravely, shifting in her seat, feeling a sense of unease at Rhona's sudden change in tone.

"You've been a bit self-obsessed of late. And before you get all 'I've been busy running a business' on me," Rhona raised her hand, preemptively dismissing any objections. "I know you have, I've been here. I see what a wonderful shop this is. You make women happy, they put on something and feel a million pounds, it's beautiful. But I need to say: you are blanking everything else, *everyone* else for that matter. Just cop onto yerself, girl." Rhona placed her hands on her hips.

"Is this an intervention? Does everyone think this?" Lori mumbled, her posture stiff as if freezing water had been poured over her.

Rhona's features softened. "Not exactly. I may be a lot of

things, Lori, but I see what's going on. And you need to give back. You have tunnel vision. There are people who need you too, who are not anything to do with your business. It's your gran's night." Rhona tilted her head to the side, frowning.

"But..." Lori struggled to find the words. Was she really neglecting people? Feeling humiliated, like a scolded child, she crossed her arms and distanced herself from Rhona. She had been dealing with a lot. Now she was being chastised for not constantly being involved in everyone's lives. Did they truly expect her to pry into their affairs? No, of course not!

Lori had been busy, and she hoped her family understood and supported her. Instead, they had been whispering behind her back, using Rhona as their messenger. All she wanted tonight was to eat a sandwich, take a shower, and go to bed. Lori was exhausted from long hours of sewing, cutting, and pinning. She had been on her feet all day, drained of energy. The thought of attending a fancy event where she had to put on a smile and engage in conversation felt overwhelming. But she couldn't say no. How could she refuse now? Lori let out a sigh, avoiding Rhona's gaze.

Rhona clapped her hands. "Oh, come on, cheer up. No one's dying. It's just a wee wine tasting!" Rhona smiled. "And don't forget, you own a friggin' clothing shop! We'll find you something to wear." She chuckled, paying no mind to her friend's subdued demeanour.

～

Lori and Rhona stood in the doorway, taking in the ambiance of candlelight flickering on beautifully draped round tables adorned with centrepieces of red and pink flowers. The cafe had been transformed into an elegant space, not a bagel or sandwich in sight! Women mingled with one another, their laughter and conversation filling the air. Waiters, dressed in sleek black tuxedos, skilfully manoeuvred through the tables, offering trays of champagne to the delighted guests. Lori was taken aback by the sheer glamour on display. She watched as sequins sparkled and shimmering ball gowns gracefully floated by. In that moment, she couldn't help but wish she had worn one of her more elaborate garments to truly mark the occasion. Her satin powder blue off-the-shoulder dress was suitable enough, even if it felt a little dated. She had made it the previous year, worn it only once and was already sick of the sight of it. The dress clung to her in ways she didn't appreciate, and she noticed the crooked stitching around the hem. The more she sewed, the more critical she became of her previous creations.

She just wanted the photoshoot to be over before she started doubting any of the new garments she had made.

Lori spotted Tammy in the distance, surrounded by women admiring little Rory, who was awake and remarkably silent, gazing wide-eyed. Lori's heart gave a small lurch. She hadn't realised how long it had been since she last saw her nephew and fought the urge to take him off Tammy's hands.

"Welcome, ladies!" Vivian, from the committee, tapped the microphone with her finger. "Can everyone hear me at the back?" She put her hand to her ear and, happy with everyone's feedback, continued. "I'd like to take this opportunity to thank you for coming. And to Miss Jay who, I'm sure you'll agree, has outdone herself with transforming the cafe into a fairy wonderland tonight." Vivian giggled. "The committee invites you to all take a seat at your designated table and the wine tasting will begin shortly!"

"Oh, how very exciting. I feel like I'm taking part in a race or competition." Rhona hooted, "let the games begin... or should I say, let the drinking begin!"

Lori examined a big board with table numbers, and when she finally found her name, realised she was at a table with no one she knew. This was all she needed. It wasn't enough that she was exhausted; now she had to make chit-chat with strangers! She made her way to the table and serious faces greeted her. Apparently, they weren't all too excited to be at her table either! She spotted Rhona some tables away near the makeshift stage and was even more disappointed to see Gran and Tammy sitting at the same table! Lori inwardly groaned and reached for the bread basket. Realising just how hungry she was, she snatched a couple of pieces and chewed them with relief.

"Save room for the cheese!" A heavy-set lady next to her chuckled.

"Sorry. I'm just starving. I don't think I've had a proper meal in days!" Lori reflected.

"Oh well, I'm sure I might not consider cheese and wine a proper meal either..." she winked. "But delicious all the same. I'm Fern, I'm new to the area."

Lori shook Fern's hand and introduced herself.

"Oh, you have that shop. I've been meaning to come in. I've been leaving it till last. I'm still exploring here and perhaps wanted to treat myself to something. I've seen your window display – stunning!" She flicked her hand. "I'm quite amazed at the quality. I hope you don't mind me saying so."

Lori chuckled. She was used to that comment from most people who came in the shop – how astounded they were to find a designer luxury brand in a fishing town in the Highlands!

"And even tonight, it's like we're somewhere cosmopolitan. I've never seen so many attractive ladies. I know it's a peculiar thing to say. Even earlier today, when I was getting coffee in the village near here, I came across a barista who could grace the cover of a magazine: her bone structure, her skin!" Fern's eyes widened.

Lori winced at the remark, knowing full well who she was referring to. Francesca seemed to turn heads wherever she went and knew it.

"But of course her boyfriend wouldn't leave her alone – texting her constantly the whole time she was making my coffee. Buzz, buzz, buzz!" Fern hooted.

Lori put down the scrap of bread and pushed the plate away. Francesca didn't have a boyfriend; if she had, it would be the talk of the town. All the local men would cry into their pints, grieving that the bouncy Francesca was no longer single – a fantasy for most of them. Lori straightened her back and smiled, remaining calm. "How do you know it was her boyfriend?"

Fern opened her mouth, detecting she may have said something out of turn.

"I mean, she may have many. I wouldn't blame her, whoever this girl is..." Lori said, shrugging indifferently.

"Oh no, she *said* it was her boyfriend. He was playing football... or something like that, on tour and she was going to surprise him with a meal. Completely smitten she was, oh young love," Fern swooned. "I guess I'm a romantic at heart. Always imagined I'd have a love affair with a Scotsman... you never know!" She adjusted her napkin on her lap and blinked. "Callum, it's a strong name, isn't it?"

Lori had been gazing at the piece of bread. "Pardon?"

"Callum, that was his name. The fellow texting the beauty," she tapped her head. "I always remember a name. I was told once by a psychic that I'd fall in love with an Alastair or a Callum, and it kind of stuck in my head. So silly, I know." Fern sighed.

Lori felt sick, her mind swimming with uneasy thoughts. After Callum's departure, she had more or less left him to his own devices, mainly so she could focus on her collection. Had Francesca been using this time to dig her claws into him? Lori stood up, a little wobbly, and declared to concerned looks from the table that she needed air. Her recent acquaintance, Fern, was already talking at rapid speed to a lady beside her about the name Alastair, too distracted to notice. Lori weaved around the tables until suddenly a wave of nausea hit her and she shivered. She momentarily steadied herself on an empty chair.

"Everything OK, madam?" a young server with rosy cheeks approached her.

She grabbed two glasses of wine from his tray and knocked them back. "Just peachy, thanks," she said, staggering out of the room.

Lori moved onward, hoping her feet knew what to do, her mind too distracted with Callum. She would have been happily ignorant and fast asleep in bed by now if they hadn't dragged her out against her will. But she was forced to face the truth behind Callum and Francesca's relationship. If she could have switched places with that parallel version of herself, snuggled in bed, content with her situation, she would. She would have switched places, especially when the cold air met her eyes, and she couldn't hold back the tears anymore.

19

"Hey!" Lori's big sister Jean called, waving her arms in the air.

Lori had been pacing along the harbour just outside her shop, and hastily wiped her tears away.

"I'm sorry I'm late. I realised I had no dressy clothes whatsoever! So this would need to do!" Jean gestured at the bridesmaid's dress she had already worn once before for Tammy's wedding. "I knew it would come in handy!" She shook her head, her hair hanging loosely around her shoulders, a different look from her usual ponytail.

"You look lovely," Lori croaked, looking away.

"Why are you not inside?" Jean frowned and caught Lori's elbow. "What's happened?" Her tone softened.

"Oh, Jean. I think..." Lori covered her mouth "I think... I m-m-made a huge mistake," she gasped, trembling. "It's not what I thought it would be... and I should've listened to my gut. I knew they weren't j-just friends," she stuttered, trying her best to stop the flood of emotions coming to the surface.

"Oh, Lolo." Jean opened her arms and Lori fell into her embrace, allowing herself finally to let the tears flow.

They held one another as the gentle sea lapped against the harbour's edge, then gradually the lapping grew louder as a large ferry approached. It dominated the view, and the two sisters watched it quietly dispatch a stream of cars.

"I think Callum is having an affair," Lori admitted.

"Oh no, not Callum. I don't believe it, Lori. You two are smitten."

"I thought we were, but ever since we came home, we've been like ships passing in the night." There was more on Lori's mind, so much more; her fear of being a mother, settling down with one person for the rest of her life and having to choose whether to have a career. But these thoughts were too far into the future to discuss. They were living with her grandmother and from the outside, appeared as housemates rather than what? Lovers, partners, soulmates? Was Callum her soulmate? He had made her happy, and they had shared a history, but shouldn't there be more? More connection, more shared interests? Maybe her calling was to start her own business, a path she may have never considered if she hadn't rekindled her love for Callum and made the choice to stay in Scotland. She had felt so sure of her decision a year ago, but now confusion lingered. If Callum was having an affair, a part of her couldn't blame him; she had let their relationship slip as much as he had.

It was all too much. The pressure was overwhelming. She faced decisions every day, not to mention her family wanted her energy for everything. Lori watched the ferry – the cars driving in a line onto their next destination – and a part of her wished she could go, hop on board, start a new life somewhere else, a clean slate with no responsibilities. She could live by herself in an even more remote place, perhaps an island? Live by the sea and sew during the day. Just her, and the waves to keep her company.

Things would be simple then.

"Come on, let's go home." Jean linked her arm with Lori's, and they strolled through the cool night air of the town. A few pubs were still open, and one of them blasted loud music. The door swung open, revealing a lively crowd dancing as a shrill voice belted out, "Unbreak my heart..."

"Yikes! Someone call the police!" Lori halted abruptly.

"Why?" Jean exclaimed.

"Someone is murdering a Toni Braxton song!" Lori quipped.

"A wee joke. Well done, you!" Jean tugged Lori's arm. "Let's go in."

"Absolutely not." Lori wriggled, untangling herself from Jean's grip.

"Oh, come on, this might take your mind off your silly notions," Jean insisted, leading her sister through the door. Ignoring Lori's hesitations, she pushed her towards a small table with two chairs at the back of the pub, nestled between a dartboard and a pool table. On the other end of the pub, intoxicated people swayed in front of the singer's emotional performance. Lori finally relaxed and wiped another stray tear from her cheek as Jean returned with drinks and shimmied off her long coat, draping it over her chair.

"It's rare you get two ladies dressed to the nines coming to this old shack. We didn't even get a double take. I'm wearing a bridesmaid's dress! But no, nothing, the barman barely even acknowledged me. All eyes are on the singer." Jean craned her neck back as the song reached its grand finish.

"I'm perfectly happy being invisible tonight." Lori took a sip of a clear drink and winced at the bitter flavour.

Jean placed her hand over Lori's. "Do you want to talk about it?"

Before she could answer, the crowd erupted in ecstasy as the woman onstage took a bow and handed the microphone to a man in a red frilly shirt, with thick blue glasses perched on his forehead. Lori blinked at his strange eccentricity, reminiscent of Timmy Mallett or some other wacky personality from the 1980s. He adjusted his glasses and read from a piece of paper, announcing another singer. A sweaty man in a white t-shirt emerged from the crowd, greeted with cheers as he pumped his fist in the air.

"I'd rather not. I'm just tired. What I need is a holiday." Lori sulked into her drink.

"Hey, you're only just back! It's me who needs the holiday – no kids, just me and a beach."

"And Karen rubbing sunscreen on you?" Lori chuckled.

"Maybe not. I think I'd rather it be just me. Maybe a Greek island where no one knows me." Jean sighed. "Wouldn't that be heaven? No big decisions apart from what I'd have for dinner, or where I would swim..."

Lori pondered on her previous desire to be alone. But perhaps Jean's version of escape was a damn sight better. "Do you want to talk about it?" Lori tapped her sister's glass with hers, breaking her out of her trance.

"I think we see things differently. It seems like everything I'm doing is a disappointment to her."

"I'm sure that's not true," Lori butted in. "Karen loves you."

"Yeah." Jean's lips tightened, and she looked over her shoulder. "Just between us two... she said so. She told me she loves me... but I..." She shook her head. "It's just getting too much. I don't think I'm moving fast enough for her. She's making big plans. And I want to slow down a bit. I need to be careful. I have the girls to think of." She pushed her drink away. "There's something else..." She bit the inside of her cheek, hesitating a few moments. "Douglas said he wants to get back together."

"Douglas said what?!" Lori cried out.

"Shhh!" Jean waved her hands and looked around.

"Oh, please, they're watching the performance of their lives!" Lori waved her hand as though swatting a fly. The MC and white t-shirt man confidently screeched a duet into microphones. Lori shuddered as the feedback pierced her eardrums. "Carry on, Jean. You can't leave me hanging!"

"OK, I've been meeting with him recently, and it's been nice." Jean smiled. "He's changed, more responsible and helping with the girls a lot more."

"But he's with someone too!" Lori bit her lip, unable to take a breath. She had liked Douglas once, but his actions the previous year had caused her sister so much pain, she'd been sure a custody battle would take place. Remarkably, it had never come to blows, and they struck up an agreement to benefit everyone.

"No, they split. He ended it. He apologised for everything."

Lori raised her eyebrow. "Everything?"

"Yes, but let's not get into all that now. It's all water under the bridge. I've forgiven him. We've had space to talk... It's been great spending time with the kids. Just us together as a family."

"Does Karen know?" Lori sipped her drink, alarmed to find it had all gone, leaving only ice cubes rattling at the bottom of her glass. She dashed over to the bar for refills, eager to get back to her conversation with Jean, until a familiar voice breathed near her ear:

"Hey, Lori."

Lori spun around, her heart giving a jolt. "Jack." She

immediately regretted coming into the pub. Seeing him tonight made her feel weak at the knees.

His smiling eyes moved over her. "Wow, you look great. Maybe a bit dressed up for the local boozer?"

Lori posed, despite her inner self cringing – Rhona may be rubbing off on her after all.

"Very smart though," he circled his finger meaningfully, "exhibiting your own work, more effective than any fashion magazine and far prettier than any model I've seen." He coughed and smiled. "That was a bit cheesy, sorry."

"Pretty cheesy, yes," Lori scoffed, leaning into him as the crowd gravitated towards the bar, pushing them closer. She ordered drinks and before she knew it, he had followed her to their table where her sister looked at her phone with a furrowed brow. "Jean, this is Jack, the photographer for the magazine shoot tomorrow." As Lori said the words, her stomach gave a small lurch. She numbly motioned to Jack and for a moment, a tightness gripped her throat; her work was going to be in the biggest magazine in the world. Shouldn't she be ecstatic? But an image came to her of what she had been like in New York: working late into the night, meeting deadlines at the last second and trying to be everything to everybody. She'd heard of fashion designers creating six collections a year, a glamorous lifestyle, but one that comprised of non-stop work.

Lori pushed those thoughts away, uncertain why they had surfaced.

Jean extended her hand gracefully, and Jack kissed it. "It's my pleasure to meet one of Lori's sisters. I hope you don't mind me joining you for a drink? I found myself at a loose end tonight," Jack announced as if he was attending some eighteenth-century ball.

"Of course not! Grab a chair!" Jean shimmied around the small table to make room, catching Lori's eye.

After several drinks, the pub had got even busier, and the three had created their own merry party. Jean and Lori had quizzed Jack on gossip about fashion models and Lori found herself relax. As the karaoke continued, she'd got into the spirit of the night, and knocked back strong drink after strong drink with a cheer.

"We should tell everyone from the wine tasting to stop by!" Jean squinted at her watch. "Holy crap, it's late! I really should go home." She screwed up her face.

"Nonsense! More drinks all round!" Lori raised her glass and hooted.

Jean bit her lip and started texting on her phone. "I suppose Karen will have put the girls to bed." She frowned. "Another hour shouldn't make too much difference."

"Hurray!" Jack clinked his glass with Jean's and brought her attention back to him. "You never told me what you do, Jean?"

The man in the wacky glasses did some very energetic motion with his hands, shushing the crowd's rowdiness. "Next up, we have sisters! Two Robertson girls who will sing one of your favourites!" He announced and scanned the audience, the bright lights shining up at him. "The Robertson sisters?"

"What?" Jean and Lori exchanged fearful looks.

"I'm sorry, I couldn't resist." Jack chuckled into his drink.

"What did you do?" Lori poked Jack in the shoulder, her eyes wide. "You're mad if you think we're going up there!"

Jean shook her head vigorously. "No way. I hate karaoke!" She hiccupped and downed her remaining drink, her chances of facing her dread were fast approaching.

"Robertson sisters over here!" Jack waved, drawing attention to their mortified expressions.

The MC saluted and declared into the microphone, "There they are. Come on up, girls!"

The crowd opened up, making a clear path to the stage. Lori and Jean walked towards the bright lights in a somewhat stupefied state, hoping that there had been a mistake and other talented Robertson sisters would appear in the nick of time. Microphones were thrust into their hands, and as they faced the crowd, it was apparent they would not make it out without singing. Lori's mouth was so dry that when the MC asked what their song of choice was, all she could do was numbly stare at Jean.

Jean muttered something to the man, and he nodded vigorously, but before Lori could work out what they had said, loud music boomed over the speakers and every face in the pub looked up at them. The beat bopped and guitar music sounded. The crowd waited. Lori reached out for Jean's hand, and they gripped one another tightly. Then Jean's shaky voice began and she nudged Lori in the ribs.

"Come on," Jean frantically whispered. "Help!"

Lori saw Jack at the bar ordering more drinks and giving them a thumbs up. She would get him back. She just didn't know how at this stage. If Jack had pulled this prank on Lori and her confident sister Tammy, it would have been a different story. Lori could have easily pretended to sing while Tammy performed the set with gusto. But Jean and Lori both possessed a certain stage fright, a shyness neither of them could shift, even as grown women. The bright lights flashed in Lori's eyes once more and unnaturally, she leaned into the microphone, ignoring the burning bile at the back of her throat. She squinted at the screen in front of her. It was a Johnny Cash song she knew well, but her eyes remained fixed on the words, her hand gripping Jean's for support. Lost in her own world, it took a few squeezes from Jean's hand to bring Lori back to reality. Opening her eyes, she was greeted by a sight that surprised her— the crowd dancing and waving their drinks in the air, showing their appreciation. She kept singing, feeling the crumpled-up version of herself unravel a little. She laughed and the bright spotlight hit her. They both moved in time, the energy of the crowd radiating back at them. And before they could sing anymore, the song finished.

"I knew you would be fantastic!" Jack put his arm around Lori and handed her a drink.

"Hmm, lucky for you!"

He grinned. "It was naughty of me." He rubbed her shoulder as he whispered in her ear. "Do you forgive me?"

Lori looked him straight in the eye, his face so close to hers she could make out a small freckle at the side of his eyebrow she hadn't noticed before. His hand remained on her shoulder. She had no intention of moving it. "I haven't decided yet."

"Anything I can do to persuade you?" He stroked her arm, gently caressing her wrist.

Lori trembled and delicious sensations ran up and down every part of her. Before she could answer, Jean pulled at her hand and squeezed through the crowd.

"Lori, we need to go. It's getting late!" Her sister grinned. "That was incredible though. Who knew we could sing? I never imagined something like that could be fun!" She giggled and high-fived a stranger's outstretched hand. "I feel like a rockstar," Jean continued, not paying attention to the fireworks that were exploding between her sister and Jack.

～

Lori staggered into her room and flopped onto her empty bed with a sigh. Jean had pushed her into a taxi before she could protest, and walked the short distance to her own house.

Apart from Bracken shuffling in the kitchen, the house was quiet when Lori turned the key. Her gran was likely fast asleep, the glamour and wine surely too exhausting for one evening. Just as Lori switched out her light and rolled over, her phone beeped. It was from Jean, her bleary eyes adjusting to the bright screen.

> *"Lori, I'm so sorry. On my way home, I saw*
> *Callum's van parked outside Francesca's. I'll*
> *call you in the morning."*

Lori flung the phone into the darkness, hearing it thump against the floor. A sharp pang stabbed at her chest as she sank back into bed. She felt paralysed, unable to sleep or gather the strength to chase after Callum. So she remained lying there, watching as the faint light of morning slowly seeped in.

20

"Don't you look fabulous!" Gran admired Lori's reflection in the mirror.

Lori turned up the cuffs on her tweed hacking jacket and pulled on riding boots over her skinny jeans. She scrunched her hair, hoping that her curls would behave today. She'd already applied mousse twice and was worried her hair was turning crispy.

"You think? I need to be warm. I might take a cape too. It can get cold in the glen." Lori carefully applied cherry-coloured lipstick, smacking her lips as she gazed at her reflection. She felt confident and looked every bit the designer she knew herself to be. Casting aside the sleepless night, she was determined to seize the day and make the most of it. Anything was possible. This was her day, and nobody could snatch it away from her.

Gran opened her bedside table drawer and produced red leather driving gloves. "Now don't these match perfect-ly?" She held up the gloves with a knowing smile. "Best to be prepared, that biting wind comes out of nowhere!"

Lori nodded and gratefully accepted the gift. Even

though they were approaching summer, she was still astounded at the pockets of cold that lurked between the hills.

"I'm so very proud of you, Lolo." Gran clasped Lori's shoulder, beaming at her. "You know exactly what you want, and I find myself in awe of your sheer drive." She pinched Lori's chin affectionately.

Try as she might, self-doubt crept over Lori. Did she really know what she wanted? She sprayed perfume, held up her chin, and made a silent vow. Today she would be strong, if not for herself, then for Gran.

Gran paused in the doorway, her frame filling the space. Her height and strength shone through, and Lori caught herself; she had spent too much time overthinking, getting distracted in the nonsense of business and her love life. All of it had caused her to forget the preciousness of her time with her grandmother, and how close she had been to losing her just the previous year. It had taken them time to restore her energy and confidence, both of which had taken a knock from the stroke. But now, Gran clasped her hands together, her shoulders eased, and she looked the epitome of health in her pink bathrobe and matching toenails.

Lori pulled her gran into a hug, holding onto the sudden gratitude that filled her heart. "It's because of you, Gran." She bit her lip, trying not to give in to her emotions. So what if Callum cheated on her? Or her fashion shoot fails miserably? Her gran would be there to support her through it, and that was worth more than anything.

Lori's green Mazda sped along the open road, flanked by towering snow-capped mountains that made her feel small.

Adrenaline surged through her veins; this was the moment, right here in the middle of nowhere, where everything would change! Up ahead, at the side of the road, she spotted Jack with his camera glued to his eye, wearing a playful smirk that hinted at some mischief in the making.

Lori rolled down the window. "Fancy seeing you here?"

"Fancy that!" He laughed.

"I heard there was to be a photoshoot here today, by a very exciting up-and-coming designer!" She grinned up at him.

"I think you'll find it's the photographer who's the big deal." Jack smirked and captured Lori's confused look with a click of the camera.

Before Lori could retort, a convoy of three black Jeeps came towards them, weaving slowly on the single-track road. Lori's stomach fluttered with nerves; *things may not be the same after this moment.* A sleek blonde with thick sweeping eyelashes and wearing a railway cap, hopped out of the first Jeep. She extended a slender, tanned hand to Jack and Lori. She waved to her stylish and serious followers but before Lori could blink, Jack had already started leading the model with her assistant down the hill towards a nearby river. The young and indifferent model nodded and took off her down coat, exposing a black leather skirt and see-through cream blouse that cascaded down to her leather boots. Lori hesitated, stuck to the spot as a few other crew members passed by her to watch the shoot begin. In between shots, the sallow-skinned model turned to get her hair adjusted and smoothed, the stylist assistant scrutinising her work with a scratch of a chin here and there.

"Excuse me," Lori interrupted the sleek fashionista from earlier, who arranged clothing on hangers at the back of their Jeep. "I thought my work was featuring in the shoot?"

Lori asked, her voice wavering as her head spun with confusion.

"Oh yes, darling." The woman waved her hand that tinkled with gold bracelets. "But we're to shoot a few other designers' work too – bit of a 'kill two birds with one stone', so to speak," she chuckled. "I'll call you when we need your costumes." She exposed white teeth, without smiling, and carried a garment bag away.

"They're not costumes," Lori muttered to herself, standing numbly. *It's fine, of course it's fine.* They would photograph her work soon; that was the whole reason behind the shoot, wasn't it?

Crew members darted back and forth to the vehicles, collecting accessories or a flask of tea for the model. Lori edged further to her car, becoming aware how ridiculous she looked in her brightly coloured tweeds and wild hair, when sleek and monochrome was the look sported by every crew member, including the model. She pushed away the doubt again. 'Costumes?', but I don't make costumes. Her overactive mind was making it difficult.

Jack, on the other hand, appeared to be in his element and fully immersed in capturing the scene. Lori observed the seamless and silent collaboration between the model and photographer. The model's playful expressions of "what are you looking at?" and "you like what you see?" seemed to beckon him nearer, intensifying his focus as he glanced over his camera, taking in both the enchanting model and the rugged landscape that enveloped them.

Lori folded her arms, leaning against her car, uncertain of whether to help or to stay out of everyone's way. Then, just before she could decide, the sleek blonde approached her, slightly out of breath. "It's time. If you could get your first costume ready, then we'll do a dress change."

Lori didn't need to be told twice. She eagerly opened the car door and handpicked the first piece she had spoken to Jack about. Their discussions about taking inspiration from the dreamy artistic paintings of Rupert Bunny had left Lori excited about what Jack had up his sleeve. She saw him crouching down, taking a side angle of the model, with bystanders nodding to one another in approval. Lori held up the hanger, and the sleek blonde clapped her hands together, commanding everyone's attention.

"Alright, everyone, time for a quick break!" She called out, and the group dispersed. The assistants continued to fuss around the model, offering support and steadying her as needed. Lori glanced at her towering high heels, realising the potential risk of toppling over if she wasn't careful. They huddled the model into the first Jeep and moments later she hopped out, half of Lori's outfit draping off her. Lori assisted with doing up the tiny buttons on the back and rearranging the folds of fabric, taking pride in seeing one of her own garments on a fashion model. As quickly as the clothes were on, Jack was guiding the model and clicking continuously, with the occasional thoughtful eye scanning the scene. Lori watched in awe, a tingling sensation enfolding her; the pieces, her own work, looked incredible. The model turned and struck a pose by a large rock, the steep hills in the distance providing a striking backdrop. This was everything she'd hoped for. She had made these outfits with her own hands, taught by her mother and encouraged by her gran.

She wished her mother was there on that barren hillside with her, anticipating the opportunities that would hopefully soon unfold.

21

Callum woke abruptly, startled by the sight of Francesca standing over him, surrounded by the soft glow of morning light. He rubbed his tired eyes, the memories of the previous night flooding back. The leaking kitchen pipes had consumed all his attention, leaving him drained and exhausted. He had barely mustered enough energy to collapse onto the sofa.

"How are you feeling this morning?" He croaked, his throat dry.

"So much better, Cal. Thanks for taking care of me." Francesca hobbled to look out the window but was fairly steady, considering. "But I think it's me who should be asking how *you* are?" She approached again, tentatively reaching to Callum's forehead. Her cool hands were soothing, but he moved his head away like a grumpy teenager – the last thing he wanted was to encourage over familiar tendencies from his friend, particularly now he had a girlfriend.

She tutted and placed her hands on her hips. "You've got a temperature, Cal."

"Nonsense, I'm fine." Callum stood up, quickly regretting the decision and flopped back on the couch. He was dizzy, and a shiver ran through his body like a wave of freezing water. He leaned his head back and swallowed, a strange tightness threatening at the back of his throat.

"You're not fine, Cal." Francesca propped a cushion behind his head.

Callum couldn't move. Apart from his limbs aching and feeling as if they were vibrating, he remained still, avoiding any further sensation. He never got sick. Over the years of putting his body under such strain, he never even picked up a cold. Francesca held a glass of water in front of him and helped him take a sip.

"Now just relax, Cal. I'll take care of you," she murmured, and pulled the curtains shut to shroud them in gloomy light.

"No, I need to get home." Callum placed his hands on his knees, willing himself to stand.

"I understand that, Cal, but you're not fit to leave, and I'm not sure I could drive you either with my ankle." Francesca grimaced. "What are we both like, eh? Just relax, and I'll make us a cup of tea."

Callum closed his eyes, angry that he couldn't be in his own bed, with Lori near. Now he was stuck, powerless and at the mercy of others, which he hated. This was a mess. He'd hoped he would be with Lori already. He wasn't sure he could endure another day away. It had been so long, and he missed her. Callum breathed in, trembling, and pulled the cover over him. Just as he faded into a fitful slumber, he pictured a dark sky littered with stars, the moon reflecting on the water and Lori dipping her head under the glassy mirror. "Lori," he breathed.

Lori stepped into her shop just as Rhona handed two large bags to a customer, sending them off with a wave.

"Holy guacamole! There's been a bit of a flurry today. So many sales, Lori!" She tidied away leftover bits from her gift wrapping. "I think at this rate we'll need more stock from our other designers!"

Lori grinned and pulled a pair of orange hand-painted earrings from the display cabinet near the entrance. "In that case, I better get these for Gran before they disappear!"

"Now, tell me everything!" Rhona crossed her legs in the swivel chair, a pen in her mouth. "How did the photoshoot go? I'm surprised you didn't bugger off with them back to New York!"

"No, darling, been there, done that, remember?" Lori said in her American droll, which came to her easily.

"How could I forget? You brought glamour back to this godforsaken empty town!"

Leanne's hopeful face popped round the door. "Did I miss anything?"

"No, not yet. Hurry up!" Rhona waved with urgency at their new arrival. "She's about to spill!"

"Where to start..." Lori frowned dramatically and paced around the front desk for suspense.

"Hurry! I'll miss the ferry! Don't leave us hanging, Lori!" Rhona leaned on the edge of her seat, sipping on a bottle of water, her eyes darting from her watch to Lori. Leanne perched on the table beside her, waiting patiently.

Lori indulged her audience by including details of the day, the people she met, the model's pouts, Jack's serious photographer face, the remarks of the sleek blonde.

"She called your designs what?!" Rhona sprayed water

everywhere, mid-sip, drenching Leanne, who brushed it off, used to Rhona's antics.

Lori waved a hand and shrugged.

"Costumes? Does she think they were for some children's party?" Leanne blinked behind her glasses, exchanging a look of solidarity with Rhona.

"Probably just a slip of the tongue. But you should have seen the peacock gown, Leanne! Your detail on the beadwork and feathers was outstanding. Oh, wait!" Lori pulled out her phone and scrolled through her images, showing her friends the proof.

"Wow!" Rhona nudged Leanne. "You guys! That is incredible!"

Leanne continued to look through the carousel of photographs that Lori had secretly snapped when no one was looking. Her face alight in wonder, zooming into each shot with a studious eye. "The colours are just..." she trailed off and handed back the phone, a dazed smile on her lips.

A wave of euphoria hit Lori. They'd done it! And what's more, those images, even on Lori's tiny phone, looked so impressive, she could only imagine how the real shots would look. She was eager to see Jack and see his work. He had left with the crew once the weather had taken a bad turn and a thunderstorm had made them stop. Lori hadn't had a chance to say goodbye. But luckily, they had photographed each garment of hers just in time before their premature departure. Now she just needed to let Jack and the magazine do their job and trust it would look how she imagined.

Lori flipped the 'closed' sign on the front door and waved goodbye to her friends. Rhona hurriedly ran in her high heels, attempting to keep up with Leanne's long-legged strides on the cobbled street. Lori unloaded her car gradually and placed all the clothes from the shoot on a spare rail, taking time to remove the garment bags and carefully check for wear and tear. Satisfied that no real damage had been done, she walked around the dimly lit shop, hands clasped, and allowed a moment of silence. The evening sunlight streamed through the front window, hitting one mannequin with an orange glow. She leaned on the cutting table and rearranged fabrics and sketches that lay scattered. The excitement from the day's events finally subsiding, replaced by a sudden furious rage. A delayed response to the previous night's findings about Callum, Lori pulled out her phone and read her sister's text.

I saw Callum's van parked outside Francesca's.

Lori clenched her teeth. She had heard very little from Callum since he had been touring the Highlands playing shinty. They may have been talking little of late, but that was no excuse to start an affair. Or maybe, Lori shivered, had she been too consumed by her business to notice they had been together all this time? She'd voiced her concerns to him many times, and each time he had insisted his relationship with Francesca was purely platonic.

She had never been able to shake the feeling that there was more to it. Their relationship had been more than close. She was sure Callum was hiding something. And now, if what her sister had said was true, he'd been lying to her. Lori threw her phone in her handbag and marched out the door with determination. One thing would happen tonight: she would finally get the truth.

22

Lori knocked on Francesca's door, while in the pit of her stomach, her intestines wrestled. Jean had been right. Callum's van was parked up on the kerb outside the house. And now she had to face whatever lay behind the door. Lori placed a hand on the outside wall, steadying herself, but her body shook with such force she couldn't conceal it any longer. A part of her was not ready to let her suspicions become true. Her body refused it, but Lori knocked again, ignoring any physical reaction.

The door swung open to Francesca's bright eyes, but her usual radiant smile faded immediately as Lori stood tall, intently waiting for an explanation.

"Lori, hi."

"Hi."

"What can I do for you?"

"Are you kidding me? Callum's been in there all night, and you think I've popped over here? For what? A cup of tea?" The joy Lori had felt earlier, now shrivelled to nothing.

"Oh, Lori, it's fine. He's just sleeping."

"I'll be the judge of that." Lori's eyes widened in a challenge, and Francesca reluctantly allowed her to pass over the threshold.

Lori didn't know where to look, she'd never been in Francesca's house, but before she could guess where the bedroom was, she came across Callum sprawled on the couch, a lumpy pink blanket draped over him.

"He's ill." Francesca stated, appearing behind her with her arms crossed.

"Lori?" said a shaky voice under the blanket.

Lori impulsively knelt beside him and grabbed his hand, which was clammy. His glazed eyes briefly flicked open, then shut again. His unusually pale face and dry lips shocked her.

Lori frowned. "What's wrong with you?"

He groaned in response.

"He woke up this way and I haven't been able to shift him." Francesca leaned against the wall.

"Why was he here? He was due to come home today." She turned away from his limp body. She needed answers.

Francesca shrugged. "I had a leak in the kitchen. It was a big job and Callum fixed it. I slipped too and sprained my ankle. He helped me. He's my friend, that's what friends do," she muttered, her posture resembling a sulky teenager.

"But why did he come here without telling me he was coming home?" Lori whispered, a frown line forming as she glanced back at Callum, who was now peacefully sleeping.

"I don't know." Francesca shrugged again. "Maybe he was going to surprise you."

Lori bit her bottom lip briefly, her rage subsiding. She looked down at the carpet floor and noticed a faint water stain around the doorway. Behind Francesca's tense frame stood the kitchen entrance, which supported Francesca's version of events. Oh, how wrong Lori had been, jumping to assumptions with no evidence. She had behaved in a way that felt foreign to her. She wasn't the jealous type, but recently she had felt erratic and stressed about her life. This was not her. Lori cleared her throat and hesitated, turning back to Callum – her first love – and she felt a weight leave her.

Her next step was obvious. She was now sure of what she wanted. He lay there, needing her. As silly as he was to be giving his time to people who just took, she couldn't be mad at him; he had been helping a friend. How could she have thought otherwise? Callum wasn't the sort of man to cheat on her, but her own insecurities had made her believe so. He needed her and she couldn't just leave him there. "Thanks for taking care of him, Francesca," she tried in her softest voice, but it came out more stilted than she had hoped. "But I'll take it from here." She rolled up her shirtsleeves and placed her hands on Callum.

"You can't take him, Lori, he's too unwell to be moved."

"He'll be fine. If I was him, I'd want to be home." She focused her attention on his pale face. "Now, Callum, put your hand over my shoulder."

"... too... heavy," he uttered.

"No, you're not, plus I did tug of war against thick headed Highlanders, I think I can move you into a car," she retorted, bending down even further.

"But, you... lost that game." A twitch of a smile came across his face.

"Oh, I see, you're too ill to move, but not that ill to crack a joke!" Lori clenched her jaw, looking Callum directly in the eye. "Come on, love, you can do it. Just get this part over and I'll have you home soon enough."

He closed his eyes for a moment, then through a deep intake of breath, he rose into Lori's grip, and slowly they made their way out to her car. Francesca followed behind, tutting disapprovingly.

Lori placed the seatbelt over the patient and laid a reassuring hand on his shoulder before closing the door and skirting around the car. "Thanks again for looking after him," she called breezily over her shoulder. "But in the future, I recommend you get your own plumber." Lori raised an eyebrow and without waiting for a response, started up the engine and drove off so abruptly a cloud of smoke erupted from the exhaust. She glanced in the rear-view mirror and saw Francesca wafting the smoke away with one hand, her face sour as if she swallowed a lemon.

Lori smoothed Callum's forehead. In the dimly lit bedroom, the curtains swayed as fresh sea air spilled into the room. She'd given him some medicine to help his fever, and he sank his head into the pillow, a slow smile across his face. Lori lay beside him, lulled by the faint breeze and his breathing. The house was still. Apart from the odd rustling of Bracken padding from his bed to the couch. Lori was relieved it was just her and Callum there. Her gran had called to say she was staying at a friend's house after a late-night dinner party. Hopefully Callum would feel better by morning...

"I'm sorry." he said drowsily. "I wanted to come home to you, Lori." His eyes opened, and he sighed out the little energy he had.

Lori couldn't find what words to say. She had been mad at him for paying her less attention of late, but was he all at fault? She nodded in response and Callum closed his eyes once again, his whole body relaxing, and within minutes he was sleeping.

As she lay next to him, listening to the slight crackle in his breathing, she couldn't help but reflect on the whirlwind of changes that had occurred. The reality of coming back home after many years working in New York was still sinking in. If she had stayed there, she may have married Michael and could have been planning their family, all the while maintaining her career. In a sense, returning home, she had to start all over again. New business, new country, new boyfriend, and what came with that? If she was to start a family with Callum, then her business would suffer. But to have children didn't mean she had to simply cease being herself, did it? She had read articles about the modern mother having a career *and* family. But surely something would have to give? She wouldn't be able to keep her hours *and* focus with a baby needing her.

Lori clicked her phone on, hiding the light away from Callum, and relived the day in her head. Examining the photographs she took, she tingled with anticipation of what Jack's final shots might look like. She must meet with him soon. She wanted to talk to him, to feel uplifted the way one could only get with someone who truly shared an interest. Who knows where she would be this time next year? It was only a matter of time when the magazine would be released and her label would be launched into the world. It could plunge her into a whole new career. And if that happened, shouldn't she grab it with both hands, rather than step back?

Lori woke with a start, her hand still clasped around her phone as Callum lay next to her, undisturbed by her sudden movement. She squinted at the screen; it was the middle of the night. She padded over to the window and drew back the billowing curtains. The cool air pricked her skin, making her shiver, and she looked up to her old friend who stared back. The man on the moon. His smile was still apparent, but this time, the markings on his creamy surface appeared darker where his smug smile used to be, which stopped Lori in her tracks. He did not tempt her or want to guide her tonight but reprimanded her like an older sibling would. The cause of such emotion was lost on Lori. However, uncertainty lingered over her. Tonight, the man on the moon lacked his playful spirit. She closed the curtain, shutting out his glow.

23

Tammy reached for a glass of water and tried to shut out the continuous crying she had endured all night. It was late morning, and she rubbed her sleepy eyes, adjusting to the new day that had already begun. She leaned over the kitchen sink, lost in her thoughts, her mind wandering again.

A sip of water made her feel worse than better, causing nausea at the back of her throat, she poured the glass's contents down the drain. She racked her brain for what day it was, could it be Sunday? The nights after the wine tasting seemed like a blur. She couldn't recall much of the conversations she had, despite seeing familiar faces and exchanging a few words. Her primary goal had been to maintain control, and she was relieved that she had succeeded, with Rory sleeping throughout most of the event. It had worked; she had shown she could do it, even though she had felt like a tightly wound coil throughout the evening. She kept going, trusting in the old saying 'fake it until you make it,' even when she felt like giving up.

After their brief night out, Rory had cried on their

return home and hadn't stopped since. Tammy closed her eyes, still hunched over the sink in an uncomfortable position, frozen to the spot, because if she dared move, she'd have to endure the heart-wrenching guilt of being a terrible mother. Rory was in the middle of her bed, screaming for attention, milk or something else that Tammy had lost the will to find out. She had to let him cry, so she could take a breather, but she couldn't escape his shrieks. They hit all over her body, confronting her with a physical reaction to hold him, but nothing she did comforted him. So she fought against her instinct and closed her eyes, and soon enough the emotion that bubbled inside came to the surface. Before Tammy could give into it, a sharp noise echoed down the hall and she spun her head around in alarm, her body seizing up at the thought of being discovered. She poked her head around the kitchen door to inspect and saw the letterbox snap shut at the front door. Seeing the post on her mat, she ran a hand through her unwashed hair, breathing a sigh of relief. After days of not showering and wearing the same pink dressing gown covered in baby spit-up, the idea that someone would check up on her would bring unimaginable humiliation.

Tammy relaxed her shoulders slightly and went back to face Rory's screams. She wondered if her neighbours heard his cries and had had enough; they could knock on her door any minute, telling her she was indeed a terrible mother and they were reporting her to the authorities. Mothers should be able to calm down their own babies. Why couldn't she?

Rory lay in the same spot of her daffodil print bed, the bright yellow flowers surrounding his chubby legs and puffy face that streamed with tears. Tammy cradled him, but his screaming didn't stop. She hushed, rocked, patted, and sang to him, but nothing worked. Each time she thought she had calmed him, he would arch his back and a new eruption of tears would begin all over again. She felt like a hamster running on a wheel, with no way of getting off and no sleep, just endlessly trying and getting nowhere. Tammy closed her eyes and rocked him, but his closed eyes oozed more angry tears and Tammy couldn't stop her own emotions from spilling out. There in her bedroom, she sobbed. She paced the small floor space, but with no more improvement on either of their moods, she sat down on the edge of the bed, feeling unbearably alone. Crying uncontrollably, she couldn't breathe or see through her blurred vision. She had thought she could do this, how stupid she had been! Tears persisted and anger flared inside her. "Why won't you stop crying?" She shouted, rocking Rory, unsure of who she was shouting at, herself or the tiny baby in her arms.

She wasn't enough. She couldn't keep this up. How could she?

In the rare moments of solitude, she would frantically search the internet for questions she already knew the answers to. However, her persistent fear always managed to overpower her: Is my baby developing normally? How long can a person go without sleep? With each wave of doubt, she found herself once again immersed in her phone, seeking answers to new questions.

Tammy's mind was a haze from the never-ending cycle of forty-five-minute sleep stretches Rory put her through. She had fallen asleep multiple times, holding him at her breast, a thing they tell you not to do in all the parenting books and blogs.

She was failing, and she was alone.

Her phone vibrated in her pocket and with one hand, she swiped it to see a message from Alan.

Didn't know if you were napping, so thought it
best not to call. There's been a delay in getting
back, love, troubles with the bus. Hotel
putting the team up for another night. I'll call
you later. Love you x

Tammy threw the phone on the bed and sat down to feed Rory again. He calmed down somewhat as soon as he nestled into her; his appetite ferocious, just like his father's. Tammy had always known that any baby of Alan's would be of the larger size, but his hunger never ceased. The last week at home without Alan to lean on had been one of the worst with Rory so far. Tammy looked back at the text message, forgetting its contents already. Alan wouldn't be home tonight. Another night without help. Tammy considered reaching out to someone, like her gran, Jean, or Lori. But the idea of admitting her struggle, of not being able to handle what they had all managed before her, except for Lori, held her back. However, Lori seemed preoccupied with her fashion business and had little time for others. Tammy sensed her sister's absence, but she lacked the energy to address it. They were in different stages of life. Tammy glanced at her phone again, hoping for any missed messages. None. Her family may be near, but everyone kept away now. The time of visiting her and Rory had lost its appeal, he was no longer a newborn, so everyone got back to their own lives.

Tammy felt an overwhelming loneliness that seemed to permeate every part of her being. While everyone else seemed to be moving forward with their lives, she felt trapped in her own self-made prison. She had even reached out to another new mother in the area, but their "coffee date" had turned into a disaster. Rory would not stop crying and squirming on her lap, while the other mother's daughter sat peacefully, gazing up at her own mother. Tammy felt the judgmental eyes of others, silently hoping she would leave the coffee shop and take her screaming child with her. In a moment of frustration, she flippantly wondered if Rory was a high-needs baby, to which the other mother nodded sympathetically, seemingly agreeing. The entire encounter was excruciating, leaving Tammy vowing to isolate herself at home until Rory became more manageable. But when would that be? The wine tasting evening had felt like a rare exception. From now on, she resolved to stay inside, shutting herself off from the outside world.

Rory dozed off in her arms and Tammy immediately picked up her phone again. *What really is a high needs baby, anyway?* She typed and soon, lost in a sea of information, she fell down the rabbit hole.

It would blow over soon. She just needed sleep. Everything would be better once Alan returned home. It just had to.

24

Over the past week, Lori had asked Rhona to cover the shop so she could spend some much-needed time with Callum. Rhona's new delivery of stock, along with her plans to create their online presence, had given her plenty of work to keep her occupied.

Callum's fever eventually subsided with the help of endless cups of tea and yummy soups and stews from Gran. One morning, as steam billowed out from the bathroom, Callum emerged, a towel wrapped around his waist and his fingers raking through his sandy brown hair. A mischievous grin adorned his face as he glanced at Lori.

"What? Just like that, you're well?" She lay on the bed admiring his form; his usual strong build had wilted a little, but Lori could see the light back in his eyes.

"Still a bit shook, I won't lie, but my fever's gone. I feel like a cloud has lifted." He shook his head in wonder, then his expression altered. "I finally have my energy back." His voice deepened, and he abruptly dropped the towel and strode towards her with determination. He leaned down to kiss her on the lips. The water rolled off him, dripping over

Lori, and she shrieked with laughter, which encouraged Callum to lean in all the more, kissing the side of her neck and the hollow of her throat.

"Oh, I see the first thing you want when you have energy!" Lori giggled, but willingly accepted his attentions.

"You can't blame me, not when you're looking like that." He moaned in her ear.

Lori looked down at her faded, oversized T. Rex t-shirt. "What?"

"You're in need of a good ravishing!" He purred and suddenly roared like an animal about to swallow her whole.

Lori wriggled free from his hold. "You've lost your mind. I'm not your breakfast!" She rolled over on the bed, making room for Callum, but he slowly sat on the edge of the bed with a sigh, pausing their game.

"All this talk of food is making me hungry. I'm famished!" He shook his head in surprise at his own words, then kissed Lori on the head briefly. "We will continue this later."

Callum, Lori and Gran lay on loungers looking over the garden. Under cover, they watched the gentle summer rain with the occasional swallow darting in between the drops to hurry home to their nests. Bracken lay in his usual position, curled up under Gran's reclined chair in a blissful state of slumber. Gran sipped from an orange dotted mug and wriggled her peach coloured toes.

"It's lovely to have you back with us, Callum." Gran smiled, raising her mug in salute.

"It's good to be back, Mary," Callum replied with a

chuckle, raising an eyebrow playfully. "But let's not make it sound like I was knocking on death's door."

"How many times? Call me Gran!" Gran teasingly scolded, taking another sip from her mug.

Lori frowned. "Well, you did scare us a bit. I've never seen you ill before."

"It was just the flu or something. It happens. I'm sure something's just going around the area." He shrugged off Lori's comment, which made her feel like she had overreacted to the whole incident. Callum had always been fit and healthy – the person you could rely on to be there. But the tables had turned, and he had needed her. Of course, people got ill all the time, but if she was honest with herself, it unnerved her. "I'll check in with the lads to see if there was a bug going around." Callum stretched out his legs with a hearty sigh.

The rain had stopped and two pigeons flew down onto the grass, bobbing their heads in some courtship dance. The three watched the birds for a while, until Gran chuckled to herself. "Ah, your grandad was the same, never ill." She smiled wistfully. "I swear I never saw him in bed nursing a cold. It just wasn't the thing, plus he was too proud. Too stubborn!"

Lori raised an eyebrow. "Too proud to be ill? That makes no sense."

"Maybe, but it was a different time. And by jove, men were different then, no offence, Callum." Gran touched his arm briefly, and Callum opened his mouth, unsure of what he was supposed to be offended about. "Jim was always running around, fixing the roof in gale-force winds or deciding to paint the old house when we had other things to do." She tutted fondly, reminiscing about their life together.

"Do you miss the old house?" Lori asked. The home they

now lived in had been her parents' and after the boating accident, their gran immediately sold her house and moved into her grandchildren's home, making various upgrades throughout the years to suit her own needs.

"Sometimes. We raised your dad there. I have wonderful memories of it. We'd spend nights in front of the fire, telling ghost stories. It was cosy. We had everything we needed." She eyed Lori with a mischievous smile. "But it was tiny, too small for me now. I like my space!"

"We're taking up a bit much of your space now." Callum casually remarked. "I bet you didn't imagine you'd have a fella moving in."

Gran's whimsical expression changed to sadness. "I'm sorry to hear you think that, Callum. I've loved having you both here – it's your home too. You're my son. You're part of the family."

Lori winced. She knew how fond Gran was of Callum, and how overjoyed she was that he and Lori were together, but he was *not* her son, Lori's father was. Callum was her boyfriend, and that alone. Of course, she was happy that her family home was the safe haven she had always known, her Gran the main reason behind it. But it had felt strange having Callum there. She couldn't put her finger on it. The pressure of the shop, the collection, and Callum had made her feel wound tight and weary, bringing out emotions she had little time for.

Callum gently placed his hand over Gran's with a sad smile of apology. The old woman shook her head and squeezed it in acceptance. Their bond was strong, that much was clear. Lori relaxed her shoulders, leaning further back to gaze up at their neighbour's rooftop. A black cat climbed with caution over terracotta slates, and, sensing the feline's approach, the dancing pigeons flew off. Lori hoped that the two birds would find a safe spot and wondered if pigeons felt their freedom, even with the risks that surrounded them. Her thoughts went to her parents, which often happened when she had a quiet moment to herself.

She focussed her attention on the wooden shed where once was a larger vegetable plot, she could see herself picking carrots with her mother and father. Pulling out a carrot from the earth and placing it in a basket by her mum's feet. Their small moments together, even if lacking in any real depth, still meant everything to her. A regular summer's day, picking vegetables together. Simple, slow, just another day. Even though Lori had aged and moved on, her parents were still there, unchanged, reminding her, bringing her back to her roots.

Reliving the moment, Lori missed the joy that growing vegetables gave her. And since Gran's stroke, they had not used the small garden as much as before. Lori loved the sweetness of homegrown carrots, or the tang of a ripe raspberry. Where once she helped her parents grow and nurture, she now just went to the supermarket. Was she missing out? Wasn't that the reason to live in the country? To live off the land? If she could carve out just a little time in the afternoons, perhaps she could re-introduce the plot. She opened her mouth to announce her idea but found Callum and Gran next to her taking a well-earned siesta, their hands still intertwined.

25

The morning sunlight streamed through the kitchen window as Lori pulled on her running shoes. The house was still fast asleep, and all was quiet. Even Bracken had retreated to Gran's door, waiting, hoping she would let him into her warm bed. Gran dismissed him regularly, but Bracken, never discouraged for too long, still tried his luck occasionally. Lori marched out into an overcast day, ignoring the light rain that lingered. She pulled her hair into a bun and hurried down to the end of the lane. Steering down onto the main road, she walked past the bakery and fought the urge to buy any sweet pastries. She persevered despite the delicious smells of glazed donuts and iced cinnamon rolls. The harbour was lively for the early hour, and on the far-off jetty, which housed a ticket office, she could make out a queue of people waiting to board a tiny ferry. The three islands on the horizon had small communities living there all year round, with the summer months bringing tourists to them to view their simple way of life. Lori had wanted to visit the islands but, for over a year, still hadn't made it over. Vowing to herself again to make the effort, she reflected that the closer one was to things, the less likely they were to do them.

She grabbed a coffee at her favourite cafe, relieved to see that Francesca wasn't there, flicking her hair and bombarding Lori with requests to fill up Callum's diary with various maintenance jobs. Lori considered the strange relationship she had with Francesca. There had never been friendship between them, and it was unlikely there ever could be. But if Callum and Francesca didn't share an old friendship, would things have been different? She weighed up the likelihood of them becoming close; going on a girls' night out, coffee catchups, enjoying one another's company. They wouldn't invite Callum, they'd have too much to talk about than to accommodate him. Lori scoffed to herself at the absurdity of it all and launched down the street at speed. With coffee in hand, she glanced at her phone, hoping for any new messages, until out of nowhere she knocked into a figure in front of her, her coffee spilling over them both.

"Ouch!" She yelled, her eyes closed, awaiting the scalding sensation that would surely follow. But to her relief, she wore a thick hoodie, which shielded her face. Her eyes opened, and she was pleasantly surprised. "Jack?"

He wiped his left arm of the coffee splatter, his eyes focusing on her properly. "Lori!"

"I thought you were back in London?" She gaped at him.

"I was, but I wanted to come and see you. The magazine is coming out tomorrow. It'll be available in the shops." He ran a hand through his wavy hair and stretched his shoulders. "I wanted to be here when it came out. I had also hoped to take more photographs..."

Lori couldn't hide her wide smile. It flattered her that someone like Jack was attempting to see her. Jack, who was going places, a 'go-getter' as her Gran would say, his openness to be near Lori left her tongue-tied. "Um, thanks." She felt her cheeks warm, holding the empty coffee cup by her side. "It's a lovely idea." Willing courage within her, she looked him in the eye. "I mean, it's really sweet of you to want to be here."

"Well, you don't seem *that* happy. I mean, you did just scald me," he jabbed a thumb at his coffee-stained torso.

"You came out of nowhere! You surprised me!"

"I've had a girl throw a glass of wine at me, but never coffee!" He raised his head.

"Oh, get away with you!" Lori waved her hand dismissively. "You're the one who stopped me from having my caffeine fix for the morning. Now what am I to do? Although, I must know more, who was this girl and can I have her contact details to congratulate her?" Lori giggled and led him back to the coffee shop. They squeezed past a parked pram through the front door and sat at a little table in the corner.

"Where are you staying?" Lori asked as she tried to get the server's attention for coffee.

"Just along the road there. The yellow door on the main street. A nice B&B. I get to wake up to the sea and the breakfast is outstanding, shame the landlady is a little... inquisitive."

Lori pressed her lips together, suppressing a laugh. He was referring to Flora Smith, the notorious nosey neighbour with whom Gran had a strange friendship-cum-arch-enemies relationship. Whenever the two women came in close contact, they would draw to their full size, like two opposing cats defending their territory, but far more entertaining to watch. In a haze of offering pleasantries, they would regard one another with an air of curiosity, admiration, suspicion and a good dollop of contempt. Lori thought back to the previous year's annual Produce Show, and how the two women competed to win the best scone competition. Her gran entered every year, and every year came second to Flora, who gloated over the losers with great satisfaction.

The coffee arrived at their table and Lori made peace with her change of plans; she would not be walking today but was delighted to be in Jack's company once again. He was a friend, one who inspired her and opened her up to possibilities. Her future could be an exciting path leading her to wherever she focused her attention. Who would have thought a tiny clothing shop in the back and beyond could attract such a flow of prospects? Lori reflected, noticing a small dimple at the side of Jack's mouth. He clicked his fingers in front of her.

"Hello. Have you been listening to a word I said?" He raised his eyebrows, his hand flying upwards. "She throws coffee in my face, then doesn't even listen to me? I'm getting a bit of a complex here, Lori."

"It's good for you. Those posh schools clearly haven't taught you a thing about self-doubt. It's a common trait for us normal people... keeps us grounded." She nodded smugly and tentatively sipped from her cup.

"Is it a big deal? That I have had a different upbringing from you?" he asked earnestly, his face moving closer to hers.

She thought about this for a moment. Once, this would have been a divide. But if her experience living in New York taught her anything, it was that everyone was equal. Of course, the world still had those problems of race, sex and privilege seeping at the edges. But with what she saw in the office, hard work was the key – if someone could do that, they could climb the ladder. It mattered very little about where you came from, more about where you were going. Since returning home, however, the gap and differences between people had become more pronounced, and Lori didn't want to spend the rest of her life choosing sides. Jack was a kind man. What privileges he had didn't change that fact.

"No, we're just from different worlds, that's all." She shrugged and changed the conversation. "Do you have any more photo shoots coming up?"

They spent the rest of the morning discussing their own plans, Jack deciding on whether to focus his attention on a painting career, and Lori considering growing her shop.

"I saw a bigger shop front down on the other side of the harbour, but I'm not sure if it's a bit too early to expand," Lori confided to Jack, who listened intently, his hand close to hers.

26

L ori clutched the magazine tightly, a whirlwind of confusion engulfing her. Had they completely messed up the dates? Standing on the street, she questioned herself, her mind a jumbled mess. Jack tried to console her, placing a comforting hand on her back, but she shrugged it off, her gaze fixed on the unforgiving pavement. How could she face Rhona, or even Gran? Avoiding eye contact with Jack, she found herself at her shop, moving on autopilot as she mechanically opened the door to a dimly lit room. The curtains were drawn shut, casting an eerie shadow. Before Lori could even begin to process it all, a sudden burst of voices erupted in unison, shouting, "Surprise!"

Party poppers burst, their bright, sparkly colours floated down, covering Lori's hair and limp shoulders. The room waited with bated breath, the spotlight on Lori. She bit her lip, overwhelmed at the crowd before her, their expectant faces waiting for her news. Rhona snatched Jack's copy of the magazine and gleefully opened it on the cutting table. In a flurry of anticipation, they popped a bottle of bubbly and filled glasses immediately to witness the full photo shoot feature. "Our local lass making it in the fashion world!" Someone shouted. With glass in hand, Rhona's hungry eyes scanned the magazine while everyone crowded around, waiting patiently. Lori watched quietly, the energy completely drained from her body, leaving her numb. She had nothing in her to tell them otherwise, so she remained still. She was to be punished for being so proud of her achievements, and that punishment was humiliation. If only she could slink far away, crawl into bed and hide under the covers for ever more.

"Ah-ha!" Rhona waved everyone around closer. "Here it is!" She jabbed her finger at a full-page image.

"Rhona, no!" Jack moved towards the table, but Lori touched his arm, stopping him in his tracks.

Unaware of Jack's interruption, Rhona held up the magazine to exclamations of oohs and ahs, the photo being of a waif-thin model standing in a glen. It was Jack's photo of the model that day.

"That's not ours." Leanne blinked at the page and cautiously watched Lori.

"Nonsense!" Rhona rolled her eyes "Nonsense!" and turned the pages to follow. It was the same model alright, and more of Jack's photographs, but exhibiting none of Lori's garments.

Lori shifted her weight from one foot to the other, dismissing the tingling sensation crawling up her legs. She tried not to focus on the negatives, but she was broken-hearted; the hours of work she had invested had been for nothing. Painstakingly hand-stitching the tiniest of details, spending all her savings on bespoke fabric, the love and passion they had put into every stitch, had been wasted.

Rhona tilted her head to Lori, waiting for an explanation, the atmosphere in the shop changed from enthusiasm to awkward sympathy.

"It's okay," Lori breathed, the words escaping her lips without her full awareness. She tried to force a smile, directing her attention solely towards Rhona amidst the many onlooking eyes. "These things happen sometimes." Chewing the inside of her mouth, she willed back the tears that wanted to come. "They used the opportunity to show other outfits, rather than run with just our selection. Magazines do this at the drop of a hat. It's no big deal." Lori's grim smile hid her true feelings, and she reached for a glass of bubbly and knocked it back in one go. She had nothing left to say. She wanted to leave, but how was she ever to leave when every familiar face looked at her with sadness? Was she to endure a conversation with each person on their departure, laughing off the whole affair with ease? She hadn't even expected an audience, which made it sting all the more.

"I'm so sorry, Lolo." Gran appeared by her side, placing a hand on her shoulder. "I know how hard you worked, but don't worry, maybe you can show them in a different magazine?" She smoothed a stray hair of Lori's behind her ear, making Lori feel like a little girl.

"It doesn't really work that way," Jack interrupted, his lips pressed tightly. "You see the photos were taken by me, under the magazine's contract. Those images can't be used anywhere else." He nodded, his posture stiff beside Lori.

Gran raised an eyebrow, examining the incomer with a hostile look. "With all due respect, young man, I was talking to my granddaughter, and focusing on the positives rather than the negatives." She nodded. "Very well, I'm sure we can organise our own photo shoot and go to the local magazines."

"Gran, I know you mean well, but no!" Lori snapped.

"What do you mean, no? It would be unfortunate to let all that work go to waste. There are plenty of other magazines out there, easier to approach and closer to home."

"You want me to stay local, don't you? Keeping to little magazines that only the local farmer would buy?" Lori scoffed. "This was my opportunity to make it... really make it. Now it's gone! I just need to accept it!" She threw her hands in the air.

"It's OK, Lori." Rhona moved in beside Gran. "As you said, these things happen. It's not a big deal—"

Lori put up her hand. "I can't do this right now. I just want to digest all this myself, but no, Rhona, you had to organise a bloody party so I have to have an audience witnessing my misfortune!"

"We're all here to congratulate you, Lori." Rhona straightened her shoulders, shocked.

"Well, I don't need congratulations. I failed!"

"Lori, stop being such a drama queen," Tammy interjected, joining the conversation. "It's not the end of the world - "

"Oh, just leave me alone. All of you, leave me alone! Can I not go an hour without one of you breathing down my neck? Live your own lives, stop following me around and trying to live through me!" Lori bellowed, slamming the door behind her. Marching down the cobbled street, sobbing into her hands, she no longer cared who saw her. She was done worrying about other people. She wanted to be on her own for once and feel what she wanted to feel.

Callum glanced at his watch as he parked his van down a few yards from *Couturier by the Pier* shopfront. He adjusted his mustard woolly hat and rubbed his icy hands together. Even though the sun glowed through the faint wisps of cloud above, he took care to keep warm. He had debated with himself all morning over whether to even show up today, for fear of spreading any sickness. But whatever he had, it had just about disappeared, only leaving fatigue in its place. He needed to be there for Lori's big day, and since he hadn't seen her all morning, he could only imagine how excited she'd be; he so desperately wanted to be part of the celebrations, too.

Hearing a door slam, Callum watched in disbelief as Lori ran past him, her face buried in her hands. She had been crying, but why? He called after her, but she quickly crossed the road and disappeared down a small laneway.

27

Bright green moss covered the top of Lori's parents' headstone, and she pulled at it, angrily dusting the matter away to expose the damp, dark stone to the sunlight. The graveyard remained as it had always been – a tranquil and secluded place where the only real differences to be found were additional headstones, a sombre reminder of time moving on. A gentle wind picked up, rustling the old oak tree above. Lori breathed in and out deeply, hoping her problems would float away on the breeze. She looked back down at her mother and father's plaque. Of course, her problems were nothing compared to being separated from her parents for most of her life. The two things were beyond compare, but she couldn't help how miserable and indecisive she was. Mentally, she felt a push inside her. At first it was exciting. Now she just felt exhausted from going uphill. It was as if her only chance was now, while she was young and free. It seemed silly even thinking about it, but it didn't make it any less real. She had failed at her chance, so what now? Time was ticking on and soon she would be just another headstone covered in moss. She chewed the inside of her mouth, a trait she'd only noticed recently, but the continuous action had left an ache. A loud noise disrupted the silence; an organ clanged, its sharp keys startling a cluster of small birds that congregated by the bell tower, their shrieks filling the air. The sound echoed throughout the glen and just before Lori investigated, it launched into a jaunty, upbeat piece of music. Over the music, a full voice sang. It was the priest, Father Angus. Lori couldn't make out the tune at first, but soon recognised it; a pop song from the 1960s era. Was it The Beatles? The Kinks? Unlike anything Lori had heard within the church walls, it suddenly transported her – she was back in the kitchen dancing with her parents. The smell of burnt toast and strong coffee hit her, the radio blaring as her parents sang and reminisced pop songs from long ago. Lori realised she was humming along.

"I thought you might be here," came a deep voice behind her.

Lori spun around, eyes wide, then relaxed immediately. Callum stood straight, his hands clasped together in a respectful posture.

He rocked on the balls of his feet. "Do you mind if I join you, or do you want some time alone?"

Lori smiled. The question itself made her instantly warm to Callum, her mood lifting.

"Sorry if I gave you a scare. No wonder, you wouldn't hear anything over that racket!" He raised his eyebrows in the church's direction, where the upbeat music had slowed right down to Debussy's "Clair de Lune".

"He's actually pretty good."

"Don't tell him that, you'll need to listen to his 'talents' every Sunday!" Callum chuckled.

Father Angus, a somewhat unusual priest, had a zest for life and passion for the arts, compared to the more sombre priests they had been accustomed to in Arlochy. He'd surprised the village by wearing sandals in winter and flamboyant scarves knitted by his beloved nieces. A champion dart player, too, he won many charity competitions across the UK. He walked to his own beat, paying no attention to the silent tuts of his more conventional partitioners. Lori liked the quirky priest, he was joyous with a wonderful voice, but she had to agree with Callum – she wouldn't welcome a longer weekly mass. Gran had already guilt-tripped Lori into attending mass, but she wouldn't be coerced into watching Father Angus sing a medley of his favourites on top of that!

"Are you OK?" Callum asked, his hand stroking her back. "I went into the shop. They told me what happened. I'm sorry, Lori."

"Yeah, I'm fine." She sighed. Whether it had been the unexpected organ music or seeing Callum's face, she didn't know, but she meant it. They stood together, lulled in the strange yet comforting atmosphere, Callum's arm around her. Then, as quickly as it arrived, Father Angus's playing stopped midway through a playful, jazzy number.

"Why did he stop?" Lori frowned.

Moments later, the bulky priest burst from the church with a phone to his ear. "What? Who is this? I can't hear you! Wait, I'll go up the hill..." Distracted with the device, he paid no attention to Lori and Callum gaping at him. His dark, balding head dipped under a low branch, and he began the ascent up the steps to where the primary school stood, along with a better phone signal. The problem with signal in the Highlands, Lori thought, was its unpredictable nature. It would come and go, blowing around the hills like fragments of a dandelion blowing in the wind.

Callum nudged her gently. "Can I show you something?"

As soon as Lori closed the van door and followed Callum up a steep hill, she noticed the surrounding elements. A stiff wind picked up and pushed against her, making her slow and heavy. The uneven ground made her concentrate on her footing, and she dodged rabbit holes along with a great deal of deer and sheep poo. She found a narrow sheep track and kept on it for guidance. As if on cue, two sheep stood at the crest of the hill, staring at them with mild indifference, their shaggy backs displaying a vivid red, a marking to say which farmer they belonged to. Lori stopped halfway, out of breath, trying to keep up with Callum who marched with ease up the slope. She shook her head. Even though he had been unwell, he was clearly far fitter than her. Determined, Lori sped onwards, finally catching up to him and meeting the glazed eyes of the shaggy pair at the summit.

"What do you think?" Callum smiled, raising his arms high. He stepped in a circle looking out to the loch on one side and hills upon hills on the other.

"I think if you wanted to go for a hike, you should have warned me!" Lori gasped, still recovering from the physical exertion, and secretly concluding that her regular walks shouldn't consist of coffee or a croissant!

"Come on, where's my wee adventurer?" He chuckled. "Not that long ago you were a thrill seeker!"

Lori had been full of adrenaline after her first deep-sea dive in Vietnam, which led on to bungee jump, then a sky dive – as soon as she finished one extreme sport, she was eager to find her next high. When it was just her and Callum, she wanted to experience everything; throwing caution to the wind, she plunged herself into anything, erasing the many years stuck behind a desk.

Lori cast her eyes down to her leather heeled shoes. "Maybe, but hiking in heels is not any girl's idea of fun!" She scanned the horizon, her breathing steadying. Clouds had cleared to expose the sea and even the inner isles. The vision so clear that she could make out tiny white houses clustered over on the nearest island. She had never been to this point before, or realised a view like this existed, capturing so many hamlets and mountains surrounding. "It's pretty incredible," she breathed.

"I'm so glad you think so, Lori" He tried to pat one of the ragged sheep, but it marched off in a huff, their meeting place spoiled by incomers.

The wind had eased, and a bright shard of sun hit them, warming them instantly. Butterflies fluttered past, darting down to the scattering of daisies on the hilltop, and Lori allowed herself to forget everything. Up on that hill, she felt a sense of peace. Nothing from the outside world mattered. It was just her and Callum again. "Can you imagine this being your view?" Lori inhaled the faint scent of woody moss, with the salt from the sea. "Waking up in the morning with a strong cup of coffee, and looking out at that." She pointed to the islands ahead.

Callum placed his hands on his hips and tipped his head back. "What a relief!" He hooted, his unusual behaviour startling Lori. "It's really important you like it... It matters what you think!" He laughed, his expression giddy. "What I'm trying to say is..." he hesitated, composing himself, "I bought it. It's ours!"

Lori waited for Callum to continue speaking, his words lost on her. She let the view distract her and her mind wandered back to the sorry affair with the magazine. Only half listening to him, she thought of how she spoke to her Gran and her friends. How could she look them in the eye again? It was only when Callum was watching her intently, waiting for her to speak, that she realised she'd missed some important declaration. "What did you say?"

"This is ours! I bought us this land. We can live here." Callum pointed to the van, his finger moving to the edge of the loch. "All the way up over the next hill." He talked quickly, Lori trying to keep up with the news. "I've secured a large section to plant a native woodland. It's so great, Lori. And we can build a house. I thought behind us would be an ideal spot, so we'll still get the view but will have privacy. Obviously I'll have trees around, to protect us from the crazy weather!" He beamed. "We'll finally have our own place, our own home, Lori."

"We have a home. My home that my parents had. I thought you were happy there." Lori's throat tightened. "Gran is there, she needs me. We're happy there, Callum. Why would you do this?" She massaged her forehead to ease a sudden dull throbbing pain in her temple.

"Don't worry! You haven't listened to my plan..." He pointed again over to another space. "I thought your gran could have her own place. I don't think she wants us in her hair, and especially if our family gets bigger."

Lori's eyes narrowed. "What do you mean by that?"

"Well, we might have kids, who knows—" He reached for her hand.

"Excuse me. Have you just planned the rest of my life for me without even asking?" Laughter spilled from her in disbelief. "I can't believe you spent money on something without discussing this with me, Callum!" She took a step back, away from him. "This is my life, too. You can't assume I'm going to give you kids and say goodbye to everything I want to do with my life! And I can't believe you think it's OK to suggest we turf Gran out to another house, leaving the house she made a special haven after Mum and Dad died..." Lori choked on her words, as fury embraced her.

"I didn't mean to... You're taking this the wrong way, Lori!"

"So now you're going to tell me how to feel?"

"Of course not—"

"Thank you. I have something of my own then!" She snapped.

"Don't you see this as a good thing? This is a fresh start. We can have our space, we have options, and we can still have your family near. I have plans."

"Well, I'm so glad you've made plans for me and my family without informing us. Tell you what, Callum, why don't you write us a letter of what you want? and we'll happily accommodate you – us silly lassies need you to make our decisions."

"Why are you being like this? I'm bloody helping all of you!" Callum retorted, then checking himself, he sighed. "Lori, this isn't you. You're taking this way out of proportion." Callum moved towards her, the palms of his hands open.

"I can't listen to any more of this. Springing this on me today as well. I just can't..." She pushed him away and marched down the hill. Tears sprang to her eyes, and she hastily wiped them away as she concentrated on the rocky terrain. Within moments, she gained enough distance to hear the calls from Callum become fainter...

28

After what felt like an extra-long bedtime story, Jean kissed her daughters goodnight and switched off their bedroom light, gently closing the door behind her. Finally alone, she breathed out; another day over. She had endured an especially tough day at school, which included more than her usual share of difficult teenagers testing her limits. She once relished teaching, even if some kids in the class made it difficult, knowing she made a difference to at least some of her students drove her onwards. Lately, though, her days had been gruelling due to staff shortages and extra curriculum expectations, so that by the end of the day she was completely drained.

Today's afternoon meeting with the headteacher, Mr Sillars, a rosy-cheeked, round man, who was once her own teacher many years prior, had cornered her with a promotion. The old man had delivered the news with such satisfaction, such confidence, that Jean had later felt guilty for staring blankly at him. Her heart had sunk at the prospect. A promotion was the last thing she wanted, but reflecting on the decision left her feeling paralysed. It would be a good career move and of course more money would be welcome, but with more money comes more work. She felt stretched thin already, without adding any more to her plate! Her mind and body remained rigid from the constant distractions of trying to achieve a work–life balance. She poured an obscenely large glass of Merlot and switched on the tv. She sipped the wine, dismissing that it was her third bottle in a few days, and gazed absently at the screen. Her body tingled, enjoying the warmth of her home and the alcohol. Then little by little she relaxed. She was exhausted, but that was the norm for a working mum, wasn't it? She pondered the idea of running a bath, but the effort to make that delight happen was too much, so she propped a cushion behind her back and laid her legs across the sofa.

"Hi gorgeous." Karen's fresh face appeared around the living room door. "Just thought I'd drop off a few things, is that OK?"

"Of course," Jean wiggled on the sofa to make room, but she couldn't even move to greet her new arrival.

Karen smiled warmly back at her, and Jean's heart fluttered. That smile was disarming. It was what instantly attracted Jean when they first met at *Adventurous Tours'* office. It wasn't long after, that Jean became intrigued and eager to spend more time with Karen's easy nature. Jean had never really acknowledged any desire towards the same sex, her only experience with passion had been with Douglas. That was all she knew. They had been together when she was in university, and once she moved back to start work, they married and started a family. It was how things were: girl meets boy, gets married, has the kids, splits from boy, then manages a stressful workload on top of family commitments. Easy! Jean had done everything that a responsible girl should. However, meeting Karen changed something in her. Not sure if the wine had taken effect, she felt a surge of desire flow through her towards Karen, wondering if she might get some release after her crazy day. She wanted to forget about everything, her responsibilities, and focus solely on her own needs. But, as soon as Jean considered suggesting the proposition, she immediately rejected the idea; with that came other distractions. She had hoped she would be alone and had little energy or interest in talking. The complexities of their relationship had taken its toll, with Karen stopping by every other night to talk, which was fine. But secretly, Jean felt her life slipping through her fingers, and she knew she had to regain control before it was too late.

Karen leaned against the door. "How was school?"

Jean sighed.

"That bad?" Karen raised her eyebrows. "This has gone on long enough, Jean, don't you think?"

"I can't change my job," Jean snapped, and a familiar silence fell over them.

Karen shifted her weight from one foot to the other awkwardly, her eyes down.

"I'm sorry. I just need a quiet night."

Karen met her gaze. "I had hoped we might talk. It's been a while since we had time together." She hesitated at the door, then came towards Jean, perching on the end of the sofa. She lifted Jean's legs up and placed them over her, her cool hands on Jean's warm feet. "I found a house. Jean, it's perfect. Enough room for us and the girls, overlooking the water."

Before Jean could object, Karen raised her hand. "Don't worry, the girls don't need to move. Well, not really. It's on the other side of the pier. It's here, Jean, it's in this town.

Nothing needs to change." She pressed her lips together with a hopeful expression.

Nothing needs to change. Jean appreciated the sentiment, but really, Karen was wrong – everything would change. It wasn't simply moving into a new house that upset Jean, it was what it meant. Ultimately, she would be announcing to the world, to the community, that she was in a relationship with Karen, which her children needed to know before anything else. Moving in with Karen also meant anything between her and Douglas would be over for good. They had rekindled a friendship which brought him back into their daughters' lives. The last meet-up had been an afternoon at the swimming pool. Both Jean and Douglas spent the session laughing and cheering at Maggie and Anne doing handstands in the pool. Jean had felt his arm rub up against hers, as they sat close together on a bench by the pool. Something triggered inside her, and she knew he felt it too. They had their history, good and bad, but he knew Jean. He knew her as a teenager, a new mother, becoming a teacher. All the big moments of her life, Douglas had been there.

She had to make a decision.

The rose-tinted vision of having her family all under one roof again, with her husband by her side, seemed like the key to making Maggie and Anne happy. She could picture that path in her mind's eye, and it felt like a safe choice. Maybe if she tried hard enough, things would fall back into place. It was the less daunting decision to make. On the other hand, there was the unknown, the woman she loved, and the fear of making the wrong decision that could jeopardise her family's happiness forever. The weight of the pressure was overwhelming, and she found it too difficult to bear.

"Well?" Karen stroked Jean's feet. Strumming her fingers

up the inside of her ankles and up to massage her calve muscles.

Jean instantly felt like jelly, and for a moment her troubles forgotten in the bliss of physical attention. "The market is competitive at the moment, Karen. They're selling houses at extreme prices, just the other week I heard the tiny cottage in the council estate went for the value of a mansion. It's crazy. Perhaps if we just wait until things cool down."

Karen shook her head, leaning forward. "This house is a bargain. I know it too. It hasn't even gone on the market. The owner would be happy to sell it to me. He's an old family friend, you see, he's selling up to live with his family in the lowlands."

That stumped Jean, and panic soon rose inside her.

"Let's take a look, shall we? I could even buy it with my money and we could work something out." She pursed her lips. "It's a no-brainer, Jean. Let's go see it, then you can decide." Karen waited for Jean's reaction, her hands placed firmly on her feet.

"OK," Jean agreed, and watched Karen's finger glide up her ankle once again. *Then I can make up my mind,* Jean mused to herself. *I hope so, I really hope so.*

29

Callum watched Lori march away from the van, her head held high, dismissing anything else he had to say. He edged the van down the drive, gazing in the rear-view mirror, hoping she would look back, but she slammed the front door without a backwards glance. Callum gripped the steering wheel. Never had he felt so powerless to express his feelings. Whatever he had tried to say as he drove her home, she ignored. He switched on the radio for a quick distraction. Perhaps it would be wise to let her cool off, he contemplated, as a 1980s pop song buzzed, the signal coming in and out in waves.

He was relieved to know that even at this awkward time, he still had his own apartment for solitude. It barely had a stick of furniture left but would be a more welcoming spot for him to rest his head for the night, than at Lori's family home.

Callum parked up outside his place and found the ginger tabby, Belinda, meowing around his backyard. He stroked her striped fur and happily accepted the simple affection she showed him by nuzzling into his hand and arching her neck in ecstasy. Callum stepped past Belinda toward his shed, which had once housed all the tools and equipment from *Adventurous Tours'*, opening its creaky door. Only a few remaining cardboard boxes greeted him. He had gradually sold or given away most of the clutter, creating more ease and space for the next phase of his life. He opened a box gently and saw women's clothing folded neatly within. He unravelled an orange hoodie, which he immediately regretted. It had belonged to his ex, Jennifer, and, just like the previous bag he'd found of her possessions; he was back in the past. A vivid memory sparked inside him: both of them under a rumpled blanket, intertwined after making love by the beach.

The wild Atlantic crashed and roared, enveloping them in its sound as they relished the cozy bliss of the back of his camper van, their own intimate sanctuary. Jennifer stretched, her movements graceful, and reached for her hoodie, a thick orange fleece that slid down her bare torso.

"What?" She chuckled at Callum's expression. "I can't just have that skimpy blanket to keep me warm."

"You have me. I can keep you plenty warm," Callum murmured in her ear, grinning.

Jennifer rolled her eyes, opening the back door to let a gust of sea wind in. Callum covered the blanket across his manhood, shielding his blurry eyes behind his hand. Jennifer climbed out and paced towards the sand, the sky a light yellow, the sun a mere moment away from rising over the distant hills.

"Isn't it beautiful," she called over just as a swell rose and another wave crashed.

"You're beautiful," Callum remarked, watching her with admiration. Her orange hood covered her hair, and her long t-shirt barely covered her upper thighs.

She turned back to him with a playful smile. "Callum Macrae, you know exactly how to get a woman into bed."

"You mean back into bed?" he asked hopefully. Jennifer ran back to their love nest, shutting the door on the waves. She climbed on top of him, and they greeted the sun, intertwined with passion.

Callum folded the orange sweatshirt and placed it back in the box. He hesitated. Unsure what he should do with Jennifer's personal items. He couldn't go through each piece if it meant delving back in the past every time. Perhaps he could give them to charity – but not every charity shop would want old brushes or half-used ChapSticks. Callum stared at the boxes; why couldn't he just do something with them? Anything was better than holding onto them! Holding onto them felt wrong – they were from a different part of his life – he had moved on.

He had moved on, hadn't he?

If he had really moved on, he could have gone through the boxes without a second thought. Callum scratched his jaw. The hurt he had gone through with Jennifer had healed, but the memories remained. If they had gone ahead with the family they had planned for; they would have teenagers by now. A boy and a girl, Jennifer had stipulated once after their honeymoon. But the time had never felt right to have children, and when she ran off with the local laird, Hector, Callum was relieved of that fact alone. But a sorrow for the same reason also lingered. He had felt alone.

Callum looked at the boxes, and Belinda, his curious companion, weaved around them. He had little time to dredge up Jennifer again. He needed to focus on Lori and explain his reasons for purchasing the land. She would come round to the idea. He may have rushed into the decision without consulting her, but she would see this would be the answer for everyone. He clicked his tongue and lifted a cardboard box, startling Belinda, who scurried away.

He knew what to do. The answer was obvious. He was owed a favour, and this time, he'd make use of it.

Lori's phone vibrated, and she scanned it immediately.

> *Fancy a drink? I'm in Morvaig, at a nice little*
> *cafe/bar next to the pier... I would love to see*
> *you. Jack x*

Lori read the words, feeling a range of different emotions about meeting Jack under the current circumstance. But he was a friend. She at least owed him her time before he left. Lori applied makeup and ran silky mousse through her hair, her curls tumbling over her shoulders. She gazed at her reflection in the mirror, studying her face and smoothing her hands across her waist. She considered for a moment how she might appear if she were pregnant. A strange thought, but would she have a full-body swell or just a neat bump like the celebrities?

She considered Callum. She knew he would make a good father, but would he be a good husband? The fact that he hid something from her, wanting to plan their life together, made her clench her fists in rage.

Bringing her attention back to her makeup, she impulsively picked up one of her rarely used lipsticks from the bathroom countertop. With careful precision, she dabbed a blood-red hue onto her lips. She pressed her lips together, then parted them, feeling her heart race as she observed her reflection. She pulled on a black fitted leather dress, which clung to her curves, making her feel sexy. She wanted to let go of thoughts, such consuming thoughts that dragged her down. Instead, she just wanted to live like she was searching for that next high. As if she were still in Vietnam, the next adventure waiting around the corner...

"Lori?" Gran called as Lori tried to sneak out the front door. "Wow, don't you look different?" Her gran gasped. "You know, I don't think I've seen you in black since you came back from New York!"

"Sorry, Gran, gotta go. Got a date!" She waved and hurried out of the house. She scrunched up her nose at her announcement of "date", hoping Gran paid little attention to the slip-up.

Lori wasted no time in speeding down the lane in the bar's direction, hoping on the way, she might have time to stop by the boutique. Approaching Morvaig town, she took a shortcut through the school and housing estate. Passing by Francesca's house, she glanced at her front door and found Callum leaning against the front rail talking to Francesca. They embraced in a hug before she led him inside, and Lori pushed her foot on the brakes, screeching the car to a stop. *What the?* She thumped the steering wheel. Rage building inside her once again. *He thinks he can control my life and then keep up this infatuation!* Lori considered her next steps and soon pushed past the need to know more. *If Callum wants to play games, I'll bloody well show him,* Lori thought, her teeth clenched, then, without a second glance, accelerated down a side road and parked directly outside the pub. Now was not the time for errands, now was the time for a drink.

She locked the car door and saw Jack's figure retreating into the pub. She followed, admiring him with a determined eye.

30

"Hey, gorgeous!" Jack's eyes widened as Lori wiggled into a booth seat. "Sorry." He laughed and crossed his arms behind his pint of lager. "I just sometimes forget what you look like until I see you. And may I say, you look absolutely stunning tonight."

Lori nodded, accepting the compliment, and took a hearty drink of her gin and tonic that had been waiting for her.

"You look like you needed that?"

"Been one of those days, yes! I need another ten!" Lori sighed, letting the day's events melt away with each sip.

"I'm sure I can help you out with that." He chuckled, his thumb sliding up his cold glass, wiping the condensation. "I wanted to see you. I'm due to leave tomorrow. I must return to London... another magazine has approached me to do a photo shoot."

Lori frowned. She couldn't help it. She enjoyed spending time with Jack, seeing his face almost every day, stopping by the shop for coffee; he had brightened up her days with his relaxed demeanour and bright smile. It hadn't hit her until now, but she would miss him. She had almost thought, or at least hoped, he might have moved to the area. He had certainly fallen in love with the place, that was apparent, his camera always in his hand capturing the next shot. Even his approachable attitude had made him popular with the locals, helping businesses he came across, giving marketing or branding advice and being paid with homemade jam or garden vegetables.

"I'm sorry to see you go," she said, mimicking his gesture and sliding the tip of her finger down her glass.

"Do you mean that?" He asked, his gaze fixed on her.

"Of course, Jack." She chuckled light-heartedly, but underneath her heart pounded hard.

"I had hoped... well, Lori, I had something I wanted to ask you. I understand things are complicated... but I want you to accompany me."

Lori almost choked on her ice cubes, trying to keep her composure.

"I think...I *know* we would be good together. What if you came with me to London? I could show you my home, my studio, you could come to the photo shoots with me. Things could really open up for you. I'd do everything in my power to help your career." He folded the corner of a napkin next to his hand. "But I do have an ulterior motive. I want to see what could be between us. I want you. All the time, I think of you."

Lori had suspected something had been on Jack's mind, but listening to his direct words had left her unable to speak. His penetrating gaze drank her in, waiting for her response. She panicked, desperately searching for a diversion, praying that something would come up—a sudden emergency like someone choking on a ricotta red pepper crostini, or a brawl erupting between drunken fishermen.

Before she could speak, Jack gestured to her empty glass. "I'll get you another." He made his way to the bar, where a young lady with her hair neatly tied up in a high bun welcomed him. She was dressed in a crisp white shirt and a tan apron, and her bright smile mirrored his. They exchanged some pleasantries, engaging in friendly conversation. Lori could see what a catch he was; definitely attractive, charming and well dressed. He was very much his own man and confident in who he was. There was a magnetism about him.

Lori regarded him as he leaned over the counter, remarking about a wine in the fridge behind the bartender. Lori couldn't resist a glance at his firm buttocks under his tight navy chinos. Desire flooded through her, causing her cheeks to flush. She quickly averted her gaze, looking down at her lap to distract herself. Desperately, she reached for her phone, hoping for a message or notification that would provide her with a reason to excuse herself. There were no messages. Nothing from Callum to explain himself; he was probably shagging Francesca by now, betraying Lori by sneaking off to hers at a moment's notice, unable to keep away from her in the end. Lori tried to shut out a persistent image that haunted her dreams and made it into her thoughts on a regular occurrence: Francesca unbuckling Callum's belt and having him on the kitchen table, the passion too intense to wait until the bedroom. Lori felt the hot temper rise within her and pushed her phone to the side.

"I hope you don't mind? I took the liberty of getting us a bottle?" Jack held up a metal ice bucket with a bottle nestled inside. The server placed two stemmed glasses on their table and gave him a flirty wink.

Lori accepted, but a small part of her wondered why

men often assumed they knew what she wanted better than she did herself.

Jack poured the wine, and an awkward silence fell over them. Lori fidgeted with her phone under the table, trying to block an image of Francesca moaning in Callum's ear.

"I can see I might have scared you," he said sheepishly, handing her a glass. "I didn't mean to. I just find myself a little tongue-tied." He cleared his throat and looked down.

"It's OK." She placed her hand on his and he took it in his palm, gently stroking the edge of her thumb with his. Lori leaned into the sensation and let her curiosity distract her. If she slept with Jack, would it really be so bad? With her relationship with Callum on the rocks, it was only a matter of time before she was alone again. Would she regret not acting on impulse? Not seizing the moment, the thrill that life had in store?

His smile returned, and he shook his sandy hair. "What I said before... I meant it. All I want, is... I want you." He edged forwards, touching the side of her face. "I'm really trying my best not to ravish you," he said, moving closer. "I dream about your lips..." He focused on her mouth. "Could I kiss you?" He leaned in. Lori remained still, hypnotised like an animal about to be devoured, lulled by the seduction. Jack moved his hand by her arm, leaning in further.

"What is going on?" Callum towered over their table. His sleeves rolled up to his elbows, his face flushed.

Jack stood up. "Excuse me?"

Callum ignored him, his eyes on Lori. "I'll ask again, what is going on?"

The tension between the three brought some looks from onlookers. The smiling bartender hovered nearby, watching the scene unfold.

"Nothing is going on," Lori said in a small voice.

"Who is this man, Lori?" Jack frowned, looking from Callum back to Lori. "Sir, you're upsetting the lady."

"I will not talk to you." Callum pointed at Jack threateningly. "Sit back down, this is between us." His serious eyes went back to Lori. "Well?"

"Callum, nothing happened. Jack is a friend. He's the photographer from the fashion shoot."

Callum ran his fingers through his hair and muttered something Gaelic that Lori couldn't catch. Onlookers from nearby tables whispered to one another with excited disapproval. Callum, hearing their hushed tones, turned on them. "Haven't you seen anyone break-up before?" He snapped, then with a look Lori had never seen before, exited the room.

Lori wanted to call after him but could feel all eyes on her. Ashamed of her actions and ashamed that even at this vulnerable time, she cared what people thought of her. "I'm sorry, Jack, I have to go." She stood up, hastily edging to the door. "Whatever was between us, I'm sorry. I shouldn't have made you think..." She swallowed. "Good luck with everything. I must go, I'm sorry." Lori left before Jack could utter a last goodbye.

Lori raced down the street after Callum, searching for his familiar stocky shape in between the throng of tourists heading in the direction of the steam train. The train whistled loudly across town to announce its soon departure, a tradition that many cherished, but not Lori. It made her teeth rattle, and now only added to her anxiety and urgency of finding Callum. She ventured down the pier and cast her eyes back towards the main street, hoping the angle would give her better visibility.

There! She saw him marching toward her little shop. Lori called out to him, but he was too far away to hear. He continued to stride forward with determination, Lori raced after him, not wanting to let him slip away for good. The steam train whistled again. Just at the same moment, Lori called out. It filled the town with puffs of white, making visibility difficult. Then, just as she ran towards her shop, she bumped into his broad frame.

"Why did you just march off like that? You've now made me the talk of the town! Nothing happened with Jack!" She blurted, her words tumbling out before she could even think what to say. Callum moved past her, but she pulled him back. "Don't go. We need to sort this out!"

"I really can't look at you just now." He shrugged her off.

"*You* can't look at me? Oh, I see, you're just going to pretend you have nothing to be sorry about -"

"I can't believe you've made this into something more than it is, Lori. I wanted the land to be a surprise for you. It was a nice thing, at least some people would think that—"

"I'm sure Francesca would have reacted better if you had offered the proposal to her. Maybe you chose the wrong girl," Lori snapped. "I will not apologise for how you've made me feel, but what really really gets to me," Lori moved in closer, "is you went back to her, after everything I said to you, you went to Francesca after our argument. Did she make you feel better, Callum? Did you finally get to have that fuck after all? Why didn't you just get together all those years ago instead of come back into my life? Or maybe I've been too distracted by other things to see you've been together this whole time?"

"What are you talking about?" Callum squinted. "Distracted? Of course you've been distracted! You've made everything about you and the shop! Honestly, Lori, you've been acting like a crazy person since we arrived home. Nothing else matters to you. I thought it would pass, but you're only interested in your own business, or whatever else you're preoccupied with – it's taking over everything.

"I'm not just interested in myself. I have my business, I have staff to pay, I need to make this a success, Callum! But now that's all gone down the toilet, I'm sure you'll be happy now."

"One setback does not mean your business has failed. Is this the reason you're acting this way? Is this why you've kept away from me?"

"How dare you put all this on me! You've been distracted too! You're always away playing a shinty match in some new tournament. Callum, you are never here, and when you are here, you go to Francesca's. I might add you have not denied your entanglement with her." Lori folded her arms, glaring at him.

"This is just ridiculous." He groaned and kicked the kerb with the side of his shoe.

"I saw you going back to Francesca's. You've made things clear... you pick her. You say pretty words to me, but you go back to Francesca. Do you talk about me? Do you laugh about me while you're fucking?" Lori wanted to hit him, the fury of everything toppling down on her finally.

He shook his head. "I went to ask Fran a favour, Lori. What goes on in your head?"

"How dare you!"

"You've said nothing about this before... you think we're having an affair? We're friends! Friends! Why would I do that to you, to us?"

"You want things I can't give you. You expect things—"

"I am not expecting things. I just want to be with you." He sighed.

Lori took a step back.

"You know what, Lori, you get whatever it is out of your system." He turned back in the bistro's direction. "Maybe once you've done that, we can talk again." Callum shoved his hands in his jeans pockets and walked away.

31

L ori walked the entire length of town. She had paid little attention to her surroundings; her focus being simply to take a step in front of the other. In doing so, she ended up in the housing estate Tammy lived in. Lori hesitated at her front door. The narrow terraced house had a small wooden fence leading towards the door, looking much the same as every other house in the estate. Lori bit her lip, turning away to walk back to the bistro where her car lay on the other side of town. Lori shuddered to herself at the spectacle she had made of herself. The whole town, and nearby islands and hamlets, would soon know. The girl who came back from New York, thinking she could open a fashion boutique and return to her old life with her high school sweetheart! Had Lori bitten off more than she could chew? And if so, why? Was it all because she couldn't quite grasp what she truly wanted from life?

Lori couldn't bring herself to leave without even saying hello to Tammy and little Rory, so she halted in her tracks. It had been a while since she had seen her sister, and she knew Gran wouldn't be pleased to hear that she had neglected her duties as an aunt. She knocked briskly on the door, hoping for a warm welcome.

Tammy opened the door, but her expression quickly changed to disappointment. "Oh, I thought you were the delivery man. I was expecting a package!" Tammy pulled her long cardigan tightly across her chest, appearing self-conscious. In the background, Rory's screams echoed through the house. Tammy rubbed her forehead, her slouched posture leaning against the doorframe, clearly exhausted.

"What's going on?" Lori walked past her in search of the noise, not stopping until she had found Rory. She found him red-faced in his crib, his arms moving in anger. She picked him up and shushed him. He took a few minutes to calm down, his cries turning to a whimper. Lori patted and swayed him until he fell asleep in her arms. She turned to her sister, but Tammy was not there. Lori gently placed Rory back into his crib, trying not to wake him, then closed the bedroom door behind her slowly. She found Tammy sat on the floor, leaning against the sofa and watching tv. Lori knelt down next to her, rubbing her shoulder. "You should turn down the tv, Tam. He'll wake up otherwise."

"Did you get him to sleep?" She sat still, her eyes remained on the screen. "I can't listen to him cry anymore. This helps me."

Lori turned down the volume, making it barely audible over the occasional car passing outside. That's when she adjusted her eyes to the dimly lit room, finding dirty nappies strewn across the floor, and cups and glasses on every surface. The kitchen on the far side of the open-plan living area showed dishes upon dishes on the countertop. The house looked like it hadn't been cleaned in weeks. Tammy, never one to shy away from work, had always been a tidy person, outshining her sisters in that respect, taking from their grandmother's domestic abilities.

Lori tried to hide the concern in her voice. "Where's Alan? Is he helping you?"

Tammy watched the screen. "He's home, but he's working in the pub and up early for the lobster catch." Her hands lay limp in her lap.

Lori couldn't hide her shock at the change in her sister, and a hot temper flickered inside her. "He's out all the time, then?" Lori had known that Alan and Tam couldn't hold on to money very well, but since the baby had arrived, there seemed to be less spending than she had ever known them to do; no more drinking in the pub, or weekends away, which had once been supported by Alan's demanding work on a fishing boat. He'd worked there for many years, sometimes staying out at sea for weeks on end.

But if they didn't need the money, were there other reasons for him being away? Lori rolled up her sleeves and immediately cleared any debris she could find. Tammy swiped her phone, occasionally looking up at the tv. Lori dried cups and placed them in the cupboard. No word spoken between them. She didn't know what to say. What could she say? The transformation in her sister was distressing; she was a shell of her former self; her face puffy and her weight loss becoming apparent after closer scrutiny.

Rory gave a small cry next door and Tammy took an intake of breath, remaining rigid on the floor. She shook her head and Lori went to comfort her, her hand rubbing her shoulder once again. Tammy choked back the tears and angrily wiped them away, then marched out of the room. Lori listened – silence. She hesitated for some time, debating whether to check on them. Then as further minutes silently passed, she couldn't endure waiting and tapped on the door. Tammy sat crossed-legged on the bed, nursing Rory. She gazed out her bedroom window, a vacant look on her face.

"I can't do this," she whispered. "It doesn't stop. It never stops." She opened her mouth as if to say more but shook her head.

Lori watched the beauty of nature; Rory was hungry, taking what he needed, but sadly removing all energy from Tammy. Her sister needed to be looked after. How had she not noticed her struggle? She had seemed confident and content as a mother – it looked effortless for her.

Lori smoothed Tammy's rusty hair off her tear-stained face. Her heart was heavy; she had been so preoccupied with her own problems, she lost sight of what truly mattered.

Lori saw the baby carrier hanging on the back of the bedroom door and, with no thought, whipped it down and secured it around her waist. Tammy handed a full and sleepy Rory to Lori as she adjusted her top.

"Rest, sis, I'll be back when he tells me to come home." She smiled, gesturing at Rory's little red head.

Tammy paused, chewing her nail. "I'm not sure. His nappy needs changed, then he might be hungry again soon." Her eyes darted from Lori to Rory wildly. "I didn't know you'd be coming. I have planned nothing for him, he might get cold..." Tammy gasped.

Lori picked up nappies and wipes and threw them into an empty backpack next to his changing table. "Trust me, Tam, I will keep an eye on him the whole time." Lori reassured her sister, then vacated the house as quickly as she could. By the time she walked to the end of the street, she looked back to see Tammy's silhouette leaning on the front gate, watching them. Lori could only imagine the turmoil her sister was going through but knew this was the best thing for everyone. Tammy needed time to herself.

Lori marched on with Rory snuggled against her chest. She glimpsed the early evening light in between the houses, and as she grew closer to the harbour, the sun hit her with full force, warming her skin. She rubbed Rory's back and gazed at the bobbing boats on the sea. A ferry left the pier, noisily chugging towards the horizon, and soon melted into the glowing sunlight.

Lori looked up at the pale blue sky, surprised to see the moon looking back at her. Early for him! She mused, curiously gazing at the milky surface for any feelings that might make themselves known to her, but she couldn't make out his expression, for he was not yet full. Lori smiled up at him, forgetting her recent problems. What mattered seemed so obvious to her now. Her problems, so small and insignificant, especially with the world moving on; time never stood still for anyone.

Even if she wanted to, Lori couldn't control her own success, love life, or fate. Underneath it all, all the words, all the actions she took...was it simply to leave a legacy? A mark of some kind, to say that she had been here after all. That she hadn't wasted her life. When her parents departed this world, they had no say in the matter, but as she approached the age at which they had passed, she couldn't help but question if she had truly made the most of her circumstances.

Rory wriggled and let out a sigh, dispelling any further self-reflection for Lori to indulge in. She rocked her hips from side to side and soon lulled him back to sleep. She hummed a tune that her mum used to sing to her when she had a bad dream, or was resisting sleep. The melody gave way to words of a nursery rhyme, which lay dormant in a Lori's memory until now:

> *The Man in the Moon came tumbling down,*
> *And enquired the way to Norwich;*
> *He went by the south and burned his mouth*
> *With eating cold pease porridge!*

Lori shook her head, still gazing at the moon above, feeling a little more connected with herself and the universe once again.

32

L ori carefully guided Rory's pram towards the shop, marvelling at him cradled beneath a cozy, knitted blanket. Lori felt a surge of love. She had taken him for the morning, to allow her sister a sleep in, but really she wanted to spend more time with her nephew. The hustle and bustle of nearby traffic had lulled him immediately into a peaceful slumber, so Lori decided to make the most of her time and check in on work.

She positioned her precious cargo by the entrance and ventured inside, only to be greeted by a sight that made her heart skip a beat. Clothes were strewn haphazardly across the floor, and her prized pieces from the photo shoot had vanished. Even items from other designers' cabinets had been hastily pulled out. Lori's mind raced, trying to make sense of the chaos before her. Had someone broken in through the open door, or perhaps Rhona had let herself in earlier and removed everything? No, that couldn't be right. Rhona wouldn't make this mess. Lori frowned and checked the cash box under the front desk, but the money was still there. Whoever had been in had run away with the stock.

Lori clenched her teeth, thinking of the expense behind the photo shoot collection. Silks from across the world and precious stones for the beadwork. Everything was unique and extravagant, but it had been for a reason. Everything was a testament to their pursuit of attention and success. If only the magazine had published the photos, they could have recouped their losses. A sadness came over her. All their months of hard work, destroyed in one swoop. She walked in further, turning back to check Rory was still in view, then exhaled slowly. She lifted a silk kimono off the floor, the first piece she made on her mum's sewing machine. It had been in the shop since its opening to the public but hadn't sold. Maybe because of the delicate fabric or the high price tag, Lori wasn't sure. It had been an education to see what did or didn't sell in the boutique. She folded it gently and placed it on the cutting table, only realising that she was moving evidence. They should inform the police of the situation immediately.

Rhona appeared behind her. Her eyes wide as she bit a pink fingernail. "What the..."

Lori wiped away a tear from her cheek, bewildered. "I don't understand. Who would do something like this? *Why* would anyone do something like this?" In silence, she made her way to the far wall, where her mother's photograph had once been. Bending down to retrieve the frame from the shattered glass, a surge of melancholy surged through her.

"I'm so sorry... I can't do this!" Rhona abruptly raised her hands. "I didn't mean to, Lori" She buried her face in her hands and sobbed.

Confused, Lori went to comfort her. "You've got nothing to be sorry about. You just came in! You're in shock, Rhona."

Rhona breathed with a slight whistle through her teeth and closed her eyes. "I am to blame. It's all my fault. I think I left the door open. I mean, I did... I left the door open." She stuttered with a nod. "I forgot to lock it last night. That blasted Sharon from the florists saluted me and I was sure she was going to chat, and you know she can talk for Scotland, so I left fairly snappish. I needed to catch that ferry – if I was late Malcolm would have killed me!" Fresh tears streamed down her face.

Rhona's outburst surprised Lori. In all her years knowing Rhona, this was the first time she had ever seen such emotion from her, even after a heated game of high school netball, resulting in Rhona going home with a fractured wrist and a dislocated finger!

"Oh, Rhona, that doesn't make it your fault." Lori took Rhona in her arms. "Whoever did this, it was *their* fault."

"I'm so sorry." Rhona pressed her face into Lori's shoulder.

"Enough of that. You've done so much for me, for the business."

"I got you robbed, that's not really doing a lot for you!" She laughed through her tears.

"If anyone should be sorry, it's me. You've given your time and your friendship. And after everything to do with the photo shoot I shouldn't have taken out my frustration on you, you were only trying to help and I took things too personally. I know you have enough on your own plate to be getting involved in my mess. I've not been... myself." Lori grimaced, still not fully digesting the repercussions of her spat with Callum.

"Oh, honey, we all get like that. The joys of being a woman. There's a lot to think about, with so much on our shoulders. If only men knew!" Rhona dabbed her eyes with a tissue and Lori caught a whimsical look in her eyes before it vanished completely.

"What are we going to do?" Rhona sniffed, pointing to the clothes and accessories strewn across the floor.

Lori stood tall and with her hands on her hips, she breathed in. "I tell you what we're going to do. You're going to make us both a strong cup of coffee, and I'll call the police before Rory wakes up!"

Rhona watched Lori carefully. "Why aren't you more mad about this?"

Lori took some moments to consider the question, and shrugged. "Because it's just not that serious. Everyone is safe, no one is hurt. Some retched teenagers will have run off to the nearest city, hiding from the law... dressed very well I might add!" Lori rolled her eyes, then couldn't help but laugh, her shoulders shaking at the daft idea of their local police officer, a pudgy older man, running behind elaborately dressed thieves waving his baton. It reminded her of a silly pantomime. She wiped her eyes from laughing and nudged Rhona playfully. "Cheer up, Rhonz, we'll get through this, we'll work it out."

Rhona observed Lori with a mixture of uncertainty and disbelief. Initially, she shook her head, reluctant to give in to the absurdity of the situation. However, Lori's persistent encouragement broke through, and a giggle slipped past Rhona's lips. In that moment, they leaned on each other, laughing uncontrollably amidst the chaos, completely oblivious to the curious gazes of passers-by.

33

F airy lights twinkled overhead and swayed in the chilly autumn breeze. The night had set in and stars clung to the sky like twinkling sequences on velvet. The Robertson family sat around a blazing fire in Gran's garden. Anne and Maggie toasted marshmallows, with wool blankets draped over their legs for warmth. Jean, Tammy and Lori sat close to the flames, reflecting on Halloween traditions from their youth.

"We used to steal the gates from all the local farms!" Jean bit her lip and whispered, "Remember old farmer MacAulay's goats went on a rampage, eating people's clothes from washing lines? They ended up looting in the school's vegetable patch. Poor Mrs MacMaster was furious. I've never seen her run so fast!" Jean pressed her lips, trying not to laugh at the memory of their stout headteacher waving a stick at the goat's behinds. "I'd kill the girls if they did that now," she muttered quietly.

"Whose gates, Mummy?" Maggie, the youngest, asked thoughtfully, keenly listening to the story the whole time.

Jean's eyes narrowed, but she couldn't shift her guilty

look. "Never you mind!" She sipped from her glass of wine, eager to change the subject.

Tammy threw her head back, laughing. She pulled her long cardigan around her and stretched her arms and legs with a satisfied sigh. With Alan looking after Rory for the night, she had agreed to a girl's evening wholeheartedly.

Lori's gaze lingered on Gran, standing on the veranda, her fingers rhythmically tapping on her phone. It was a sight that caught Lori off guard, her gran rarely used the device. She casually slipped it into her skirt pocket and leisurely made her way towards the crackling fire, cradling a newly opened bottle of wine. The cool breeze picked up and ran along Lori's arm. She snuggled into a patchwork blanket, pulling it closer around her. The air was calm, just like her mood.

"Now you know I'm not one for speeches, but I have an announcement to make." Gran stood, looking down at her family, a strange look on her features.

Lori knew better than to laugh at her gran's favourite way to start a speech. She said it so often, Lori had lost count of how many speeches her Gran made.

"It's been a busy year for us, hasn't it? A difficult year, some may say. But we've got through it, together." She watched Maggie blow on a hot marshmallow, her fingers pulling at the sticky whiteness. "Anything is possible when we have each other. I love you all. I hope you know that."

Lori frowned. "Gran, is something wrong?" Her voice unsteady, fearing her gran's health problems had returned.

"Not at all!" Gran hooted and shook her head. "No, let me put that notion to bed. There's nothing wrong. I've got plenty more things I want to see and do. It's actually some exciting news I've got to tell you... There's to be a wedding!"

Lori and Jean exchanged confused looks.

Gran squinted at her watch just as the doorbell rang. She shimmied off, humming to herself.

"Gran, don't leave before you've told us who's getting married?!" Tammy shouted after her gran's retreating figure, but with no reaction, turned back to her sisters. "Is it you and Callum, Lori?"

"He'd need to talk to me first and I don't know if that'll happen again." Lori pressed her lips, dismissing the heaviness weighing on her heart.

Jean opened her mouth just as a guest appeared in the doorway. A tall man, slightly stooped but with an air of sophistication about him, wore a suit jacket over a brown knit jumper. His thick grey hair was combed back to show sideburns. Gran beamed up at him and chuckled at something he had said. He nodded toward the girls, their audience, who gaped at them.

"It's Mr Green," Lori whispered to her sisters and shifted uneasily.

Jean gasped. "What the grumpy Mr Green who made Gran's committee a nightmare?"

"The very same," Mr. Green said, appearing close to the fire, startling them all.

"We didn't mean..." Jean recoiled. "We just didn't know you and Gran were... um... friends?"

He smiled bashfully.

Lori's eyes narrowed, immediately feeling the responsibility of the family on her shoulders. She would not allow this man to have it easy, especially after how he spoke to Gran in the past. It wouldn't be right to accept his words without reprimanding him first, if there was one thing you could say about the Robertson family: they didn't take crap from anyone.

"Well, it's nice that you are friends, but you didn't make

things easy. You weren't particularly approachable... and on many occasions, you were pretty vile to Gran. You tried to embarrass and humiliate her. Now you've changed, have you?" She breathed in, controlling her emotions before they got the better of her. But she couldn't keep quiet. "I must say, Mr Green, you were very unkind. Gran has always put this community ahead of everything, and you accused her of using the area for her own gains. I recall you calling her a—"

"Lori!" Gran hushed her granddaughter.

"She's right." He touched Gran gently on the elbow and shrugged. "I said that. And I am mortified at how I behaved. I've apologised to your gran since then. But I see I owe you all an apology, too. I would never talk to her like that again. Never. She is my angel." He closed his eyes, looking at the ground, before fixing his attention on each granddaughter. "I'm sorry for any hurt I may have caused. I let life experiences haunt me for too long... that they clouded my judgement on others. Life had withered away to dust until I met her." He turned to Gran. "Mary, you saved me. You brought me back to life, and for that, I'll be eternally grateful." He took both her hands in his, his eyes reddening.

"Aw," Tammy sighed, betraying her sisters, and Lori nudged her.

Lori and Jean looked at one another in astonishment, unsure what was unravelling before them.

Tammy sat up. "Gran, you said there was to be a wedding?" She waited on the edge of her chair, her hand tightening around Lori's arm beside her.

"Oh yes, where is my mind?" She tapped her head and shook it gently. "Lawrence and I have thrown all caution to the wind... as some might say. We've decided to get married."

Lori gulped, her throat dry. "What? But you don't like each other?" The words fell from her mouth before she could stop them.

Gran and Lawrence eyed one another, then erupted into fits of laughter.

"But I'm so confused," Tammy pulled Lori close and whispered in her ear.

Jean leaned in beside her sisters. "You and me both!"

Gran wiped her eyes with a tissue from the amusement and popped it out of sight underneath her sleeve. "No, we didn't like one another. But things change, we change. Nothing stays the same in this life, that much I know from my long years in it." Gran gazed at Lawrence. "He makes me happy. That's the truth of it."

Lawrence kissed her hand, and they held on tightly to one another.

"It's just... a shock!" Lori shook her head. "But of course we want you to be happy, Gran." Lori looked from either side to her sisters and stood up. "Congratulations!" She held out her glass that had remained clenched in her hand and toasted the happy couple. It wasn't long before they were opening another bottle of wine and watching the fire flames dance into the night sky.

34

The sun beamed down the next morning, making nature thrive unusually late for the time of year.

"It's like a summer's day, the last we'll see until next spring," Gran mused by the kitchen window, as if knowing the weather to come. She sipped green tea from a china cup, lounging in a cotton dressing gown. Lori snapped into action, venturing out with a towel over her shoulder, eager to make the most of the day. She sought her favourite secluded beach and lay on the sand immediately. Her fingers dragged across the fine sand and her feet wriggled under the sun's warmth. She let the sun melt away her worries. Having spent too long worrying over things she could no longer control – Callum, the shop, her gran – she had left it up to fate.

She heard distant calls of geese as they all made their way from one field to another, grazing and settling near the water. Lori sat up and crossed her legs, gazing at the horizon. The water shimmered in the sunlight, inviting her in. She cautiously looked about her for any onlookers but being so late in the year, many of the tourists had gone, leaving the whole beach for her. She took off her shirt, exposing a small bikini underneath, and tentatively went to the sparkling water. Daring to do a spot of snorkelling, she fastened a mask around her head and dipped her toe in at first, and amazed at its warmth, soon plunged into the crystal-clear sea. She swam, stretching her legs behind her, kicking her further and further out towards a rock that jutted out of the water like its own little island. She had never been out as far before, but felt confident in her swimming abilities.

After promoting Rhona to co-owner of the shop, Lori had taken a step back from the business, focusing solely on designing and creating, while Rhona took care of sales and marketing. Rhona, excited about her new role, immediately hired Leanne part-time, which had eased both their schedules immensely. Everything had all fallen into place, with Lori gaining back some more precious personal time in the process and since spending less time in the shop meant less coffee and more walks each day with Rory. She had more energy than she ever knew.

Lori perched up on the rock, admiring the coastline, and stretched out, lapping up the sun like she often saw the grey seals do. She studied the deep turquoise water below. A golden carpet of white sand lay at the bottom. Not too far down, a glittering pearl light beamed up, and she squinted at it, wondering what it could be. Some treasure thrown overboard long ago? Lori took a deep breath and dived towards the light. She reached out to grasp it, but it disappeared. She dived further towards the sand but couldn't see anything. The strange light had disappeared. Frustrated, she swam to the surface, hoping that she hadn't overlooked a secret jewel of the sea. Flicking her heavy wet hair away from her face, she pulled off her mask, adjusting her eyes to the sunlight, but encountered a smooth pointy surface heading right for her. She shrieked and pushed it away before it knocked her head. Confused at what was happening, she hadn't realised that it was a kayak she had pushed with force into the jagged rock. Callum, the driver, momentarily distracted watching the coastline, shouted something inaudible, before quickly losing his balance. The kayak crashed, and Callum flipped into the water with a splash. Lori watched in alarm as the kayak remained upside down with no view of Callum. She took a deep breath, about to plunge underneath to find him, but before she could, the vessel rocked. Moments later, Callum gulped for air nearby. He shook his head and wiped his face.

Lori resisted the urge to swim to him, realising she was the reason for his boat capsizing. She remained floating in the same spot.

"Hi." She smiled awkwardly. "Are you OK?"

"What happened?" Callum held onto the kayak but remained in the water.

"I sort of pushed you into a rock... by mistake!"

"Of all the seas in all the world, you swim into mine!" He ran a hand through his wet hair, which had grown since Lori had last seen him.

"I'm sure that's from a movie." Lori rolled her eyes. "And excuse me, you don't own any of the seas!" Lori didn't know how to speak to him. The memory of their last fight came back to her, disrupting her mood.

Callum stared at her, coming to his senses. "What are you doing here? Why are you this far out?" He looked back at the beach.

The sun had drifted behind clouds without warning, and Lori shivered. "It didn't seem that far," she mused, but regretted the earlier decision as her limbs were getting tired in the salt water.

"Seriously, of all the places I'd think to find you – this was the last place." He looked away back at the beach. "I thought I'd get some space to think."

"Well, I'll leave you to think. I must be going," She said brusquely.

"Don't, Lori, here take this." He moved the kayak towards her. "I'll swim back, you're clearly cold." He swam towards the rock island and helped her into the narrow seat. She steadied herself and accepted the paddle. He pushed her ahead. "Race you!" He shouted, then started swimming in the beach's direction.

Lori couldn't help but laugh and easily paddled out in front while Callum speedily kept up. Back to shore, she pulled the kayak up onto the beach and sat down, exhausted. She lay back on the sand and closed her eyes.

Drops of water landed on her feet, then carried up to her face. Callum stood above her, looking down.

"Looks like you fell asleep." He chuckled through a heavy breath. "And before you say it, I wasn't that far behind you!"

Lori's mouth twitched.

Callum flopped down next to her, his breathing gradually slowing.

An awkward silence fell between them. Lori didn't know what to say. It had been weeks since they last spoke. Their parting words had been so sour that she felt paralysed how to move forward. She wanted him, but there was too much between them, and she felt exhausted figuring out where to begin.

A gaggle of geese echoed across the sky, and they both gazed up to see them glide overhead, heading southward.

"Have you seen any dolphins today?" Lori broke the silence, hoping to distract him with small talk.

Callum shook his head. "All calm out there, not much wildlife... apart from some herons. And the geese, of course, no doubt they'll be off to some place warmer."

Lori dusted the sand off her hands. Reaching for her towel, she placed it around her shoulders, shielding herself from the wind.

"You're still cold?" Callum asked with concern. "I'm sorry."

"You've got nothing to be sorry about, it was me who tipped your boat over!"

"Kayak," he corrected.

"Whatever." Lori sighed.

"I meant, I'm sorry for what I said." He cast his eyes to the lapping waves, their foam edging over the sand towards them. "I've been thinking about us and what I said to you... I've been waiting for you to come back to me, but you didn't. Whatever happened with Jack, I don't want to know. I just want to know if it's done, and you'll come back to me? Will you, Lori?" He turned to face her, his jaw set.

Lori sat still, her hands submerged in the sand.

"I'm worried that I've failed you. You're the last person I want to hurt."

"You haven't failed me," she breathed. "I just feel pressured."

"Have I pressured you into something?"

"You decided what you wanted from life and that I would automatically want the same thing. I feel so much is expected from me." She paused. "I don't know what I want... but I don't want to be led down a path without my consent."

Callum opened his mouth, then shut it again.

"I know you think I overreacted. Maybe I did a little. But

I know I don't want to be pushed into a life I didn't sign up for." She clenched her jaw. "I had that in New York... with Michael. I can't accept that... I refuse to be dictated to."

"I don't want to control you, Lori. I love you for who you are. I thought you knew that."

Lori shrugged. "I do, I guess. I'm just scared."

"Of what?"

She pulled the towel around her shoulders, hiding her trembling body. "I'm scared my life will turn into the mundane, and I want something extraordinary. Seeing Tammy... Rhona... I don't want that life. I hate myself for even saying it, but I don't want to blend in, become a mother and wife, and hide behind a family... my identity lost forever. Everything I worked for to disappear." She bit her lip, unable to meet his gaze.

"I'm sorry you feel that way." He looked down, unable to meet her eye. "I think being with you has made my life extraordinary. I know we are meant to be together, Lori. Why would you think I want you to become a faceless person?" He frowned, looking at her directly. "We don't need to do anything you don't want to." He hastily ran his hand through his hair. "How can I make you see? I would do anything for you. I want to be with you. I want to make you happy."

"At the risk of me not wanting kids?"

Callum blinked, taken aback. "What?"

She shrugged again. "Maybe I don't want kids. I don't know right now. What if I want my career over having kids? Or what if we decide to have kids, and we can't have them... or if we have them and I end up resenting them for taking away everything from me!" She shook her head and frantically wiped away a tear. "I can't ask you to be with me. You clearly know what you want. I don't... not yet anyway."

Callum sighed. "Is this the real reason you've been distant?"

"You've been distant too," she said defensively.

He reflected for a moment. "I have, and I'm sorry for it."

"And all that bullshit with Francesca?"

"How many times must I tell you? She's a friend, that's all!"

"I'm tired of this. Of all of it." Lori looked away. She was done with going over the same arguments with Callum. She stood up to leave.

Callum jumped to his feet. "Lori, please don't leave. I won't see Fran again, if that's what you want?"

Lori looked back at him one last time. "I don't want any of this." She moved away from him, leaving only her footprints on the beach.

"I only want you," Callum said quietly to her retreating back.

35

J ean clasped her palms together and placed them between her knees. They were clammy because of her fretting, but it was time. She had to be straight with Karen. She dipped her head in anticipation at the reaction she was to face, feeling like a dog waiting to be reprimanded by his owner. She couldn't look Karen in the face, desperate to have their talk over with immediately, but knew she couldn't rush it.

"What? I thought we were happy with the house?" Karen's confusion met Jean's resolve, and they both sat opposite one another at the kitchen table. After eating a late dinner, Jean saw an opportune moment to discuss her hesitations once they had put Anne and Maggie to bed. She had Karen's attention fully; there was no backing out now. "This is our big chance to become a family," Karen frowned.

After they had viewed the house, Karen had struck a deal with the owner, shaking hands on a price. Apart from the paperwork for them to sign, it was theirs by verbal agreement. Jean had felt a strange elation, like being on the edge of a cliff, excited but terrified of what lay below. She couldn't stop shaking all over. It was only when she had a cup of tea several hours later that her nerves finally had settled down. But now, after some time to adjust to the idea, she felt only terror.

Jean held her tongue. She already had a family. "I told you I needed more time. I have the girls to think of."

"What you really mean is you're scared," Karen immediately snapped. "I know you, Jean, you're copping out because you don't want anyone to know you're gay!" She shook her head angrily.

"You know I don't like labels, Karen."

"I know." She paused, then trying a different tack. "You're letting other people dictate how you live. You see that, right? You're doing what you think you need to do, but who's it all for?"

"My girls," Jean answered.

"Oh, come on, we live in the 21st century, there's gay people everywhere. Your girls don't care about that."

Jean gave her an exasperated look.

Karen took Jean's hand in hers, ignoring her sweaty palms, searching her eyes. "I love you."

Jean replied, "I love you," and meant it.

"Then why can't we announce it to the world?"

"I'm not ready."

"Will you ever be ready?" Karen sighed. "I love the girls. I want us to all be together."

Jean shook her head. "I can't move in with you. I need to put them first. They need as little turmoil in their lives as possible. They had to go through all that trouble with Douglas and me splitting up. This is their time. They need just a bit of calm. They deserve that much."

Since Jean and Douglas had resolved their previous misgivings, she had come to see her girls in a different light.

In a way, she felt closer to them, as if a door had opened. She couldn't understand the reason behind it. Maybe it was having their father around more, or that they were growing up so quickly she didn't want to miss any moments. Whatever it was, their bond was as strong as ever.

"You can't wrap them up in a cotton wool blanket and keep them protected from the world, Jean. Don't you want them to take on the world confidently? Be raised to accept people for who they are, to love themselves, even if they don't fit in the mould of what people expect of them?" Karen pursed her lips. "We would raise them to be comfortable in their own skin. We would be strong together and love them unconditionally. That's all that matters."

Jean rubbed her eyes wearily. "It's all too soon, Karen. Why do you need to jump on these things? We need time to see where our relationship is heading."

"I can't sit around and wait for you to fall out of love with me!"

"I will not do that. Honestly, Karen, it doesn't need to be all or nothing. I don't have that luxury to go from one relationship to another, without thinking of the consequences of who I'll be hurting, there's more than just us two in this."

"You think you're doing it for them, but you're not, you're doing it because you have no backbone."

The words stung like acid. "That's not fair. I know what it's like to have my world ripped from underneath me and have to face it alone."

"You can't compare this to losing your parents, Jean." Karen's tone softened. "I can't imagine what it was like to go through that pain, but this is different."

"I was Anne's age." The flashback hit Jean, bringing her back to the day she heard the news of her parents' tragic accident. She had started her period that morning, too

young to know what was happening and too afraid to tell
anyone. She hid her underwear, terrified that she was about
to die, just like her parents. The guilt and grief consumed
her for days, until Gran had taken her aside, after finding
the evidence, and explained everything to her. She had
Gran and her sisters, but those years had been her introduction to womanhood, and she couldn't accept not having her
mother there to guide her.

"It's not the same. You must see that."

"I know it's different, but at least I have control over this
situation. I know what I feel in my gut, and it's telling me to
slow down." Jean recoiled, moving her body away from
Karen's outstretched arms; she must shield herself and keep
her emotions in check. If she focused on her daughters, it
made the process easier. She just needed to keep them in
her mind's eye. Tears streamed down Karen's face, and Jean
resisted the urge to comfort her. This was what she expected
would happen. It would either be resolved or over. The
outcome would be here soon.

"I can't believe you're throwing all this away. What we
have is special, and you're choosing to be alone, just like that
little girl who lost her parents. You don't need to do this,
you're choosing it to be that way. I hope you realise what
you've lost." Karen slowly stood up. Then, with no further
words, no desperate pleas or apologies, she swiftly left the
house, quietly closing the door behind her to not wake the
girls.

Jean stared ahead. With her palms no longer clammy,
she placed them face down on the table, as if she were about
to stand up. Her heart pounded and she could hear the
blood thump in her ears. The house was still. Thankfully,
her girls were asleep. The last thing she would want was for

them to overhear a break-up of a relationship they didn't understand.

In the morning, she would take them to the swimming pool and get a bag of chips on the way home. She would give them her full attention and spend the whole day together, just the three of them.

And if she was strong enough, she'd tell them they wouldn't see Karen anymore. And they would be fine. Everyone would be fine.

Jean dug her fingernails into the kitchen table and took a deep breath in, but it was no good. The tears came too easily and within seconds; she sobbed uncontrollably.

Tomorrow she would be strong, but right now she let herself fall apart when no one was looking.

36

Tammy showed up at Gran's house unexpectedly and threw her bag on the kitchen table with abandon.

"What's up?" Lori asked. The slightest American drawl still persisted in her voice, which Tammy teased her about from time to time. "Where is Rory?"

"Rory is with Daddy today," Tammy eyed her phone, "at least for the next hour. So we need to make this quick... I have a surprise for you!"

"Oh, really?" Lori was intrigued, but the last time Tammy had surprised her, it had been about her pregnancy and the affair with the local laird. She shook the flashback away. It was all water under the bridge now. But she still was dubious about Tammy's tone; her manner unsettled her.

"Come on, I ain't got all day!" Tammy coaxed her sister out to her little car, then as soon as she closed the doors, she swore aloud to herself. "We need to get you a change of clothes, something warm to wear... It might be a blizzard tonight!" She bit her fingernail.

"Where are you taking me, Tammy?" Lori asked wearily.

"Oh, you'll see. Now, wait right here!" She ordered and marched off back into the house.

Lori's mouth opened in quiet question. Should she immediately leave the car and wait in the nearby pub, at least until Tammy had left the scene altogether? She knew her sister would be furious and would track her down eventually, but she might have some time to herself before they released the search party. Lori groaned and reluctantly decided her best option would be to await her fate anxiously. She clicked on the radio for distraction and a dated song crackled loudly. She sighed. It seemed the local radio station had the same song on repeat.

She chewed her fingernail, anticipating what was to come; maybe Tammy was taking them all on a girls' night, or maybe it was something to do with Gran's hen party? Lori hoped, but her optimism faded as she remembered her gran's last comment on any pre-wedding celebrations. "Excuse me, I'm not a hen!" She tutted and made Lori promise to never mention it again. Lori sighed to herself, attending Gran's hen party would be far more preferable - wearing matching fluorescent pink crowns and necklaces adorned with penises, as they eagerly watched Gerry, the part-time stripper and part-time fisherman, perform his lively dance routine.

Tammy trotted out with a stuffed backpack over her shoulder, carrying a loo roll in one hand and a thermal coat in the other.

"Where the hell are you taking me? Camping in Iceland?"

Tammy frowned, contemplating something, but started the car anyway. She slammed the brakes immediately, and they both rocked forward with force. "I've forgotten something. I know I have!" She placed her hand on her forehead.

"If you tell me where we're going, maybe I can help?" Lori smiled. "It's OK, you know I hear 'baby brain' happens to most mothers..."

"Oh ho, I'm not falling for that one, nope, you'll just need to make do with what I packed!" Tammy pushed the throttle, and her little car skidded down the drive and on to the main road, the radio crackling loudly.

Much to her disappointment, and without warning, Lori had been ordered to wear a blindfold. Tammy's stern eyes studied her until she reluctantly put the black eye-mask on.

They continued on and Lori lost track of how long they were driving, but soon Tammy switched off the engine and escorted Lori outside. The cold wind whipped around her and she shivered.

"Where the bloody hell are you taking me, Tam?" She shrieked. Tammy didn't answer, and to Lori's alarm, she heard the car leave, but before she could whip off the blindfold, it was removed by big hands. Callum. His frown greeted her.

"I don't know why you have a blindfold on," he said sheepishly, "that wasn't part of the plan."

"I thought for a minute she had done a deal with the CIA and I was the bait!" Lori shook her head, adjusting her eyes to the gloomy light. They were on a hillside, with water on one side lapping at the edge. It was the land Callum had bought, the cause of their fighting. "Well, are you going to leave me here shaking?" Lori demanded and snatched the winter coat he held up, irritated with the whole charade. "Shall we get on with this?"

He led her around the hillside on a path covered in wood shavings, softening their steps. They turned a corner and Lori gasped at what she saw. A wooden hut was nestled next to a small burn that trickled down to the shore.

Lanterns were dotted along the pathway, their glow leading up to an oval shaped building. It looked like a child's playhouse, but far more luxurious than any Lori had ever encountered. Two small windows showed warm light inside with tiny tea lights on the windowsills. They walked up wooden steps which led onto a small veranda. Lori glanced back at the view. The day had edged into dusk already, and a mist covered the water, skimming its surface and closing in on them.

Inside the cabin it was cozy and welcoming, with a basic kitchen on one side, and a low couch and cushions by the fireplace. In the centre of the room a log fire blazed. A table in the far corner displayed a banquet of food. Callum pressed his lips tightly and rubbed his hands together nervously.

Lori examined the room. "It's like the beach hut in Vietnam?" Her words stuck in her throat, remembering their special nights alone off a secluded island.

"Inspired by." He nodded. "I wanted to take you back there, but I didn't think you would have come on the plane with me – I don't think Tammy's skills would extend that far!" He chuckled awkwardly.

"You made this place? By yourself?"

"Yip." He rocked on his heels, then gestured for her to sit on the sofa. He opened a bottle of wine, pouring them a glass.

Lori shifted on a cushion, sitting cross-legged. "I don't know what to say."

Callum breathed out for a moment and bowed his head as if summoning up energy. "I don't want you to think I've brought you here to trap you and make you listen to me. You inspired this place, and I wanted to show you it. I had hoped I could build it, but I didn't really know. I doubted myself and almost didn't do it. But I thought of what you'd say and so... I kept going. You were with me every day, motivating me to keep going."

Lori's cheeks flushed, and she hoped the dim light concealed it. "It's amazing, Callum, you should be proud of yourself."

"I am." He smiled.

Lori took a sip from her glass and relaxed her shoulders a little. "You've been really busy—"

"I've missed you," Callum cut in. "I'm sorry, Lori, I can't waste time with small talk. You know me." He smiled grimly. "I want you. Can you ever forgive me?"

"It's not that simple." She placed her glass down on the floor. She wanted him, too. Of course she did. But there was too much between them to detangle. Ultimately, they wanted different things. Or at least that's what she felt.

"I think it is that simple. You're playing with ideas of what might or might not happen. You've created a narrative in your head that I'm going to hurt you, or vice versa. We don't have to know where we're going, Lori. All that matters is we're going there together."

"What if we give this a go and I realise I don't want kids? Then what?"

He shook his head and turned to the fire, grabbing another log and wedging it in. "I never really told you much about Jennifer, my ex."

"I know she hurt you badly," Lori hesitated, choosing not to delve further into the painful details. She was aware of Jennifer's affair and how quickly Jennifer and Callum had become involved after Lori's departure. They had been married for a long time, and a part of Lori couldn't help but feel like the second choice when it came to Callum's affections. If Jennifer hadn't betrayed him, perhaps they would still be together.

He shrugged. "She did, not completely for the reasons you may think. But I feel I need to be honest with you. She said she didn't want kids. I was disappointed, to say the least. I had assumed we would, we had talked about it once...she was great with children. Then our parents were always asking, 'so when are you going to start a family?' I was gutted, but I had to respect her decision."

"And it may be the same for me," Lori whispered.

"I know that. But she went on to have kids. It was *me* she didn't want to have kids with. That was the real reason. She chose to have that affair with Hector as a means of breaking us up. And if that's the case for you... please tell me and I will let you go."

Lori observed Callum's body language, noting his folded arms and lowered head. He seemed so vulnerable, and her heart ached for him. "Oh, Callum, it's not like that for me, not at all," she said softly. "I want to be with you too. I just... I don't know what I want."

Callum's gaze locked on hers with determination. "I want you, and you want me. There's nothing more to say," he declared, his voice steady and resolute. "Whatever comes our way, we'll face it head-on." He reached out and gently held her cheek. "I love you," he whispered.

Lori felt the weight of the moment, and without hesitation, she said, "I love you too." The realisation hit her with full force, and all the doubts and complications seemed to fade away. It *was* that simple. Why had she made it so complicated in the first place? Tears welled up in her eyes as she blurted out, "I'm so sorry. I shouldn't have said all those things. I couldn't bear the thought of putting you through..." Her voice trailed off, her apology hanging in the air. "I've

just been so confused about everything. I don't know why..."
She stopped, her hand to her mouth. "I can't believe I tried
to push you away..." She shook her head, tears streaming
down her cheeks. "Please stay by my side."

"I wouldn't dream of leaving," Callum said, a smile
spreading across his face. He took her in his arms and kissed
her tenderly.

Lori gazed out at the Milky Way as it trailed across the
speckled night sky. The wind had ceased, and the moon
reflected on the loch before them. Callum appeared behind
her, wrapping a large blanket over the two of them. He
kissed her hair, breathing in her scent.

"It's a full moon," he whispered in her ear.

"The man on the moon," Lori mused, gazing up at her
old friend.

"Or the woman on the moon." He touched her neck
gently, his breath near her ear. "The moon feels like a
woman, always has done for me."

Lori reflected, perhaps he was right. Perhaps they were
both right.

"You know, as mad as it seems, I always thought she was
smiling at me." He chuckled, squeezing her shoulder.

"She's smiling at both of us tonight," Lori reflected
whimsically. A sense of trust and optimism lit up within her.
She knew then deep within herself, everything would be
alright.

EPILOGUE

Gran walked into the living room to her waiting audience. "Will I do?" She opened her arms, turning around on the spot confidently.

"You're a vision, Gran," Jean declared in between the statements of approval from her sisters.

"You've pulled it out of the bag, another success, Lori. This is truly exquisite work!" Gran smoothed her hand over her hip and took a bunch of roses Jean had been holding for her. The pops of pinks, yellows, and oranges made her smile. "I love colour," she mused, then remembering something, popped out of the room briefly to come back holding a pair of high heels in hot pink. "I had to add a little touch of me!"

"Well, I said I could've made you a multicoloured dress!" Lori raised her eyebrows.

"Not at all." Gran waved a hand dismissively and popped on her bright shoes. "I wanted to feel like a bride again." She looked at her reflection in the living room window, the gloomy winter wind thrashing against it. "It may seem silly, I know, but the first time was so joyous. I loved being a bride. It's different this time, I know. I'm a good fifty years older now..." she trailed off, with a tinge of melancholy in her voice.

"Fifty years wiser," Jean offered.

"Fifty years more beautiful." Tammy stood beside Gran and laid a hand on her arm affectionately.

"Fifty years more *you*, Gran." Lori smiled. "This is your day, and we're so happy for you and Lawrence."

Gran wiped a tear before it fell and chuckled, opening her arms to all three of her granddaughters. "My wee women. You are my world." She embraced them and a peaceful stillness kept them locked together tightly. Bracken stood close, trying to nuzzle between their feet until Gran clapped her hands. "Now away with you all before my mascara runs wild and we force Laurie to marry a snivelling woman."

Lori waited by Gran's side outside the church, and a gust of wind made Gran's dress billow up high. Alarmed, she pressed her skirts back down frantically. "I feel like Marilyn Monroe. Let's hope the church isn't as draughty!" She joked, but Lori could feel her trembling next to her.

Dressed in a tailored suit, Lori had refrained from wearing a dress and instead followed Jean's example by wearing trousers for the big day. She took the place of her father to lead Gran down the aisle, an honour she held onto tightly. Lori pulled away from her own inner thoughts and peered around the door to see the congregation listening with rapture to the talents of Father Angus. With ease, he rattled through a medley of Gran's favourite songs, his voice and organ work effortless. Lori reflected on the previous organist who couldn't hold a note, relieved that it was the priest who was performing for the crowd. He slowed down, then his head popped up over the organ to salute Lori. He began his rendition of "Unchained Melody" by the Righteous Brothers, and Gran nodded to Lori. It was time. Still shaking next to her, Lori pulled her in close and led her slowly down the aisle. They passed familiar faces, each reflecting unbridled joy.

"That Father Angus, he's a one-man show," Lori muttered. Gran playfully nudged her and pursed her lips, trying her best not to burst into laughter down the aisle in front of everyone.

Midnight arrived, and they made cheers for the New Year. Gran had secured a jazz band and a ceilidh band, both of which were now playing a mash-up of Ella Fitzgerald and a Highland fling.

The guests made a ring around the village hall, clasping hands to sing "Auld Lang Syne" as was the tradition for Hogmanay. They jauntily moved into the middle of the room to then abruptly swing around one another in ecstasy. Once the music came to a stop, Callum and Lori welcomed the pause for refreshments. Perched at the end of the bridal table, Callum gathered Lori in his arms and kissed her.

"Goodness me!" Gran exclaimed, appearing with a champagne flute in hand, accompanied by a beaming Lawrence by her side. Lori reflected on how he gazed at her grandmother, like she was a queen bestowing her love on a mere mortal. Her heart warmed all the more. Her gran exhibited a confidence she had never quite seen before, always comfortable in her own skin, but tonight she radiated like someone fully at peace. "These lovebirds! What do you think this is?" Gran chuckled playfully. "A romantic occasion?" She clasped Lawrence's hand tighter.

"They seem very taken with each other," Lawrence said awkwardly. "You leave the young kids alone, Mary."

"I should think they are taken with one another!" Gran teased. "Do you know they were high school sweethearts? I always knew they would get together again."

"What? Even when I lived in New York?" Lori raised an eyebrow.

"Most definitely. It was just a matter of timing."

"These things usually are." Lawrence's gaze moved from the young couple back to Mary. He kissed her hand and led her towards the dance floor.

"Well, maybe she's right. You are the best man I know, Callum Macrae." Lori shrugged.

"And you, Lori Robertson, are the best woman I know. Well, apart from your gran, of course!" He winked at the bride, who had stayed momentarily within earshot, waving coyly. Lawrence held her close, and they waltzed together with ease. Callum placed his hand over Lori's. "I let you go once. I'll never let that happen again. We're meant to be together, Lori. You have always been in my heart and always will be."

Lori placed down her wine glass and turned to him. "Well, if that's the case, maybe we better make it public, then?" She surprised herself. And before she could take the words back, she realised - she didn't want to. She straightened her shoulders, waiting.

Callum's shocked expression met her challenging one and soon they both smiled with an understanding.

"Maybe we will." He pulled her in close and whispered something in her ear, making her laugh aloud.

Guests waltzed slowly nearby underneath glimmering lights, each with hopeful acceptance for the year ahead.

WANT A LITTLE EXTRA?

Head over to www.clairegillies.com to receive a FREE download of Lori and Callum's high school meet-cute.

THANK YOU

If you enjoyed reading this, please leave a review on Amazon and Goodreads...and tell your friends! It really helps new readers discover my books.

Thank you so much lovely reader.

Claire x

AFTERWORD

As a new mother navigating the pandemic in a foreign country, writing became my lifeline. It was the one thing that connected me back to myself and gave me comfort during those challenging times. It was during this period that Lori's story came to me. I wanted to challenge society's expectations of women and explore what really happens after "happily ever after".

You know the one - where a couple comes together, everything is lovely, and the story ends neatly tied in a bow. But we all know that's not how real life works... I wanted to take a realistic look at the pressures that modern-day women face and the daily juggling act that comes with it. It's not always easy, and it's certainly not a neatly tied package like in fairy tales...

Revisiting Arlochy surrounded by its familiar faces and the sense of belonging, brought me such joy. The image of cherry blossoms in full bloom and the scent of sea air lingers in my mind, along with bleached white cottages lining the bay eagerly awaiting my arrival for the summer. I hope that you, too, can feel the warmth of their welcome embracing you.

I'll be returning to Arlochy again soon and hope you'll join me...

ABOUT THE AUTHOR

Claire Gillies writes heart-warming, uplifting women's fiction set in Scotland. Having grown up in the Scottish Highlands, Claire later lived in Australia for several years, working in retail and creating her own fashion label.

Now back in Scotland, Claire resides in beautiful Inverness-shire with her family. She finds inspiration in her love of folklore, costume, and history, which infuse and shape her writing.

When she's not writing, she indulges in her love for costume dramas like Poldark and Jane Austen adaptations, by curling up on the couch with a cup of tea.

Claire enjoys connecting with her readers on a personal level. Sign up to her mailing list and grab some goodies at www.clairegillies.com

Join the conversation!

ALSO BY CLAIRE GILLIES

From Scotland with Love

On the Edge

ESCAPE TO THE
ORKNEY ISLES...

CLAIRE GILLIES

"Wonderful
feel-good book
with humour &
heart"

on the
edge

OUT
NOW

Milton Keynes UK
Ingram Content Group UK Ltd.
UKHW010835240823
427277UK00004B/37